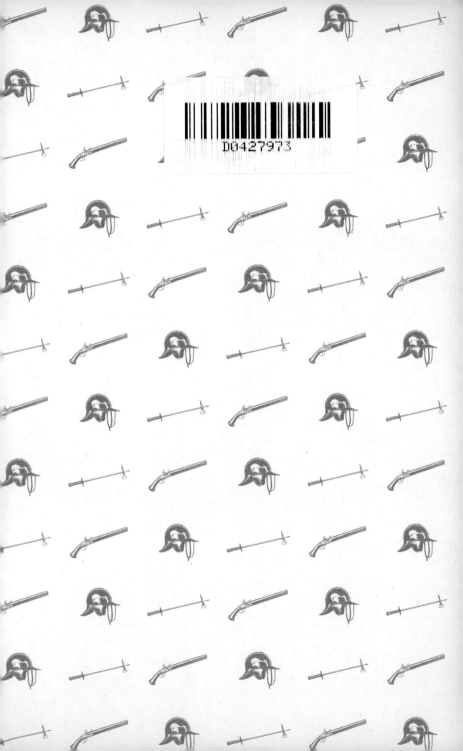

D0427973

Troublesome Thomas

Jenny Sullivan

Pont

Published in 2007 by Pont Books, an imprint of
Gomer Press, Llandysul, Ceredigion, SA44 4JL

ISBN 978 1 84323 811 9

A CIP record for this title is available from the British Library.

This book is published with the financial support of the
Welsh Books Council.

Printed and bound in Wales at
Gomer Press, Llandysul, Ceredigion

With all my love to
Kieran, Hon. Grandson, and the twins,
Izabelle and Cassidy, Hon. Granddaughters;

Daisy Antonina Ruth (Daisy Roo) granddaughter
and
Louis Breckon
a.k.a. 'Thomas'

Foreword

This novel, like its companion volume Tirion's Secret Journal, is set at Llancaiach Fawr Manor, Nelson, South Wales.

If you visit Llancaiach Fawr with your family or your school, you will certainly meet some of the people mentioned in this book. However, although Bussy Mansell had a son named Thomas, he would not have been ten years old in 1645 – Bussy himself was only 22. So I've taken a bit of a liberty with his age, and also that of Colonel Prichard's elder daughter Jane, who was only 7 in 1645, and not 10. She was also probably a perfectly nice little girl, and not at all the way I've depicted her.

So, when you visit Llancaiach Fawr Manor, you will definitely not meet Thomas. The servants there will know absolutely NOTHING about him, so it's no use asking!

Throughout the story you will find little numbers in the middle of the sentences, which refer to bits at the bottom of the page. These are called footnotes, and although they may not directly have to do with the story, they are Interesting Bits and Pieces about the Seventeenth Century, and Thomas and I wanted you to know them.

My very grateful thanks to everyone at Llancaiach, especially Dot Harvey alias 'Elizabeth Proude, Seamstress', who has been amazingly helpful.

The story begins at Bussy Mansell's house in August 1645 . . .

Chapter One

'You are an exceedingly wicked and troublesome boy, Thomas,' my tutor said. 'You must be punished, and once again you most thoroughly deserve it.' His nose twitched happily. 'But rest assured, Thomas my boy, that beating[1] you will most certainly hurt me far more than it will hurt you. In punishing you, I myself suffer in a manner scarcely to be borne.'

That's what he always says, that it will hurt him more than me. Do I believe him? No, I certainly don't, but that might have something to do with the smirk he always wears when he says it. Anyway, he took off his coat, rolled up his sleeves and gave me a good whacking with his special cane, the whippy one. I'd really like to think it hurt him – that would make me feel much, much better. But I don't expect it did. I think he enjoys it. Whacking me is probably the only exercise he gets.

---

[1] Badly behaved small boys were often beaten – in posh families like Thomas's usually by their tutor. At school they were beaten by the teachers, and probably by older schoolboys too. It probably didn't make them behave any better, though!

Master Prisiart, my tutor, is very old. Prissy by name, prissy by nature, that's what I think. Mind you, behind his back I call him Wartnose, for reasons which should be obvious. Despite his great age (he must be at least thirty), Wartnose is quite strong. While he's whacking away at the seat of my breeches, he has a sort of ritual – he recites this poem, a line between each whack:

> Whack! *First I command thee God to serve,*
> Whack! *Then to thy parents duty yield.*
> Whack! *Unto all men be courteous,*
> Whack! *And mannerly in town and field.* Whack!

If he doesn't feel he's punished me properly by the time he gets to the end of it, he recites it all over again – and sometimes again – until he thinks I've been whacked enough. Today he got through it seven times, and I wouldn't like to tell you how my poor bum feels.

Old Wartnose was a master at a school for boys before Pa hired him to be my tutor, and according to him the boys at his school were *always* beaten twice a day for absolutely nothing at all. He said it helped to keep them in order. Pa (whose name is Bussy Mansell, and he is a very brave soldier who is fighting for the King) says Wartnose is not allowed to beat me more than once a day, and then only if I deserve it. The trouble is, Wartnose seems to think I *always* deserve it, so my bum is sore more often than not! I could go and complain to Pa, but he's usually very busy, and anyway, grown-ups always believe other grown-ups, so it wouldn't do me any good, and Pa doesn't like complainers and tell-tales, so I can't win, can I?

I don't think I deserved it today.[2] I was trying to keep out of Old Wartnose's way, true enough, but you'd have done the same, if like me, you sort of hadn't got round to learning your Latin by heart. It was five pages of some boring old book with crabby, cramped black writing – so I knew I was in for a thrashing. I wasn't trying to avoid it, no chance of that – just to delay it for a while, and have a bit of fun while I was doing it. I was hiding up a tree in the orchard, which is as good a place as any: besides, I

---

[2] Children then were exactly the same as children nowadays. They just wore different clothes and didn't have Playstations and X-Boxes and stuff. But in those days, all their faults were looked on as Really, Really Awful. This made some abnormally well-behaved children act like horrible prigs. One lady, writing her diary later in life, said that as a child, she was made to play with children she loathed, and she would keep on telling them how to behave. However, she goes on to say that she also pulled all their dolls to pieces, so perhaps she was fairly normal after all!

like trees. Wartnose was looking for me, and shouting my name, and threatening me with all sorts of punishments – as if that would make me come down and meekly trot out to take my whacking! I could hear him off in the distance, round the front of the house, thrashing the shrubbery with his stick.

And then, as I peered through the branches, I saw something that made me sit up and take notice, all thoughts of Wartnose and Whacking driven right out of my head. A stranger was creeping through the orchard. I kept very still and quiet and watched him. He was dressed all in black, and he definitely looked furtive and suspicious and most certainly Up To No Good. He was walking sort of bent over, almost crouching, as if he was trying to hide! It struck me like a bolt of lightning: this must be an evil, wicked Parliament spy,[3] sneaking about to spy on my pa! After all, everybody knows everybody around here – and this man was a stranger. Everyone knows that strangers can't be trusted, don't they? Sometimes, even people you might think of as friends can't be trusted, not in wartime. I heard Pa say to Ma that some people changed sides whenever the wind blew

---

[3] In 1645 the King and Parliament were on opposite sides, fighting a Civil War. (That means people of the same country fighting against each other.)

from a different direction. He was angry because he'd just had word that Major Kyrle of Ross, who was in command of Parliament's forces when they beat the King at Pontrilas, came over to the King's side, then went and treacherously changed sides *again*, and betrayed the town of Monmouth by foul trickery. If there are evil men like that, even in command, no-one can trust anyone – and now, here was this bent and suspicious-looking Stranger creeping through our orchard! He was Up to No Good; I could feel it in my bones!

My heart sort of went thump! and my stomach gurgled – but that might have been starvation – I hadn't eaten anything for hours, not since breakfast. What if he had a knife or a pistol, and had come to shoot Pa dead as a stable rat? (With the pistol of course – he couldn't very well shoot him with a knife, could he?) I had to stop him somehow. But I'm only ten – and I didn't have a sword and anyway I usually just fight with the village boys and my fists – quite a lot – and usually get whacked for it.

I watched him come closer to my tree, and closer – and just as he walked underneath, I got up all my courage and determination, and jumped out, right on top of him, smack! I landed on his back, squashed him to the ground, and sat on him, hard. Then I held on while he struggled and jerked and shrieked, and I screamed and screamed too, for someone to come and help capture him. And I bounced quite a lot, too, to make sure he stayed squashed. Old Wartnose came running.

But I got it wrong, didn't I? As usual. He wasn't a Parliamentary spy at all. He was the new Baptist Minister, come to call on Pa, and he wasn't creeping suspiciously; he always walked like that – there was something wrong with his back that made him walk all bent over. How was I supposed to know?

Now, *I* think, and I expect you will agree, that trying to stop my Pa getting assassinated by a wicked spy isn't something a person should get punished for. You might call it an honest mistake that anyone might make. But nobody else thought so, unfortunately.

So as well as getting whacked by Old Wartnose, I also had to go and see Pa. I ask you, is that fair? Getting punished twice for the same thing? No, I don't think so, either. Pa was bound to think up something to really make me suffer. Whackings hurt while they are happening, but then they are over and it's all forgotten until the next time – which isn't usually very long, with Wartnose in charge. But Pa's punishments last longer – one time he stopped me going into the village for three weeks! He said until I could learn to behave like a gentleman, I had to stay at home and study instead. It was awful. I had to sit indoors for days reading boring old Latin and Greek. I couldn't do anything – not swimming in the river, not chasing the village girls and putting spiders and worms down their necks, not stealing fruit from the villagers' plots, not guddling[4] for fish in the river – none of the things that make life worthwhile. I had to stay at home and do extra lessons with Wartnose instead.[5]

I waited in my chamber for Pa to send for me, sitting on a fat cushion because my bum was sore. I hoped I'd still be going out later on with Tomos Potsiwr[6] when suddenly there was Old Wartnose, wearing an ugly expression as if trying very hard not to smirk: he was trying so hard that the big fat wart on his long thin nose was twitching. 'Master Thomas, your dear father will see you now.'

---

[4] Guddling is a lovely word, isn't it? It means lying on the bank with your hand in the water. When a fish comes along, you wait until it swims into your hand and then you whip it out really quickly – and there you have supper!

[5] Boys learned much, much more than girls, whose education usually stopped quite early. Richard Evelyn, who died of 'six fits of the quartan ague' aged five, when he was only **two** 'could read perfectly, in English, Latin, French and Gothic letters, while at the age of five he had a 'strong passion for Greek'.

[6] Poacher.

Oh, wonderful.

Pa was standing in the withdrawing room looking Very Stern and Very Serious. The new Minister had been pacified and apologised to, and probably given a glass of wine, and then he'd taken his leave and gone back to his Ministering, I expect. I went and stood in front of Pa, with my head down. It wasn't done to look him in the eye when he was angry with me. That was classed as being Bold, and I should certainly get whacked again for it.

'Thomas, I cannot begin to understand your behaviour. How a son of mine could behave in such an appalling manner, so viciously attacking a poor – '

'But, Pa – ' I wanted to explain that I had been trying to save him from being murdered by a Parliament spy – well, *I'd* thought he was, anyway.

'Don't interrupt, Thomas. Behaving in such a discourteous manner to a man of the cloth.[7] I shall not be able to look the poor man in the face again. A member of my household, behaving so unforgivably. What were you thinking of?'

'Pa, I was – '

---

[7] Man of the Cloth means a Vicar, or a Priest, or any Clergyman.

'I said, don't interrupt, Thomas. The poor Minister was battered and bruised, and the breath was entirely knocked out of him. All the same, he was determined that you should not be punished – '

He was? Really? How come Old Wartnose whacked me, then?

' – but I promised him that I would see to it that you learned the error of your wicked ways. Thomas, you must learn to control your behaviour.'

'Pa, I really – '

'You are interrupting again, Thomas. I have decided that on this occasion your behaviour warrants extreme measures.'

Oh Beelzebub's bum![8] This sounded serious. Three more weeks of Latin? A whole month?

'I have spoken to Mama, who agrees that your actions were appalling. Attacking a visitor to – '

'But, Pa! I – '

'Don't dare interrupt again, Thomas! Attacking a visitor to our home, bouncing around upon the poor man's head and shrieking like an inmate of Bedlam![9]

---

[8] Beelzebub is another name for the Devil . . .

[9] 'Bedlam' is a short form of 'Bethlehem Hospital' which was a lunatic asylum. Posh people used to wander along and watch the poor, unhappy, mentally-ill people – for entertainment. Not very kind, was it?

The poor Minister might have died of shock! Your punishment – '

Oh dear.

' – well, Mama and I have decided that you shall be sent away for a while.'

My mouth fell open. I was being banished? Just because I had tried to save Pa's life?

'Wh-where, Pa?' I managed to squeak, thinking, *oh, please, not away to a school!*

'To your Aunt Prichard's[10] home at Llancaiach Fawr. And there you shall stay until I decide you may return.'

'But, Pa, I – '

'And that is my very last word on the matter, Thomas. You are a most troublesome and ill-behaved boy, and I hope that dear Aunt Mary, and your cousins, little Mary and young Jane, will use their gentle ways to civilise you. Now, go to your room and collect your things together. I have sent word to Llancaiach Fawr to expect you. You and your tutor will leave tomorrow.'

---

[10] Bussy Mansell, Thomas's father, was Colonel Prichard's brother-in-law, which means that he was Colonel Prichard's wife's brother.

Chapter Two

It was no use arguing: I knew perfectly well that whatever Pa said, Pa meant. He never says 'maybe' or 'perhaps'. No good pleading with Ma, either. Ma never goes against Pa's wishes, not ever.[1] So that was me done for – the following day, I had to leave Breton Ferry[2] and go to visit my aunt, Mary Prichard, and her husband, the Colonel.

I had never visited them before, and didn't know my uncle at all, although Aunt Prichard and my cousins visit us quite often. From what my aunt says, the house she has at Llancaiach Fawr is not one bit as grand as her uncle's home at Breton Ferry. Aunt Mary, being Pa's sister, was a Mansell before she was

---

[1] Ladies didn't, not in those days. They might sulk a bit, but they certainly didn't argue. Wives who argued could be beaten with a stick no longer than the man's forearm, and no thicker than his little finger.

[2] Yes, Breton Ferry. Not Briton Ferry, as it is today. Apparently, once upon a time it was used as a crossing place for Breton people coming into Wales from France. Perhaps when England began fighting France (which they did in the olden days, a lot) someone decided it might be a good idea to change it! French people weren't very popular in those days.

a Prichard, and she bleats on about Breton Ferry's twenty-three hearths and fireplaces, and grand rooms and wonderful gardens while behind her back, Ma rolls her eyes. I overheard Ma say once that if Aunt Mary ever stopped complaining about Llancaiach, she'd probably die of boredom! Aunt Mary says that Llancaiach is quite grand, and at least has an indoor jakes,[3] which seems very nice to me, but that the house is cold and draughty and she is forced to sit all winter with her feet resting on a footstool filled with heated coals just to stop herself freezing to death. Perhaps if she moved about a bit, she wouldn't get so cold.

I think perhaps Aunt Prichard is just one of those people who are fond of being discontented, and to tell you the truth, I wasn't looking forward to staying with her at all. And as for Mary and Jane – well, Mary is too little for me to notice, but Jane . . . I would have difficulties with Jane, if I had to live with her. She is a prig. Jane says that I am noisy, dirty and uncouth – and so of course I try extremely hard to be all three as often as possible whenever she comes to visit! But then she complains about me to my tutor or to Pa, and I get whacked again. I am not

---

[3] Or loos, privies, toilets, House of Commons, bogs, and many, many other names!

fond of Jane, even if she is my cousin. But then, you don't *have* to like people, just because you are related to them, that's what *I* think, don't you?

Next morning, early, we set off, Wartnose and I, in the farm wagon driven by Dai Snaggletooth, because even though Ma wept and wailed when I left, and said that Pa was being harsh, and that I was a poor, wayward, misunderstood lamb, she still couldn't spare the carriage. Pa had already sent a messenger[4] to warn Aunt Prichard that we were on our way, so we weren't likely to get sent straight back because there was no room.

It was a long journey, especially sitting on a hard wooden seat in an uncomfortable, jolting cart, but at least it was the end of August, and dry, and also I didn't get sick – although it was a near thing once or twice. I'd much rather travel by horse, but Old Wartnose doesn't ride well, probably because he is so old, and so I must suffer instead of him. We broke our journey at an inn halfway. I was quite excited by this. I'd always wanted to stay at an inn and see lots of drunken people, and perhaps fisticuffs and brawling and suchlike, but no chance of that,

---

[4] Perhaps a man on a fast horse, or maybe even a message by carrier pigeon – no telephones or email in those days, but the birds were fairly fast!

unfortunately, because Wartnose bundled me straight up to our room and made me stay there. Mind, *he* went back down to the taproom and came back much later with his breath smelling of wine. Loud shouts and women laughing and all sorts of interesting and intriguing noises drifted up the stairs, and I watched from the window in case there was a fight, but there was nothing outside but some run-down stables and a stinking midden.[5] Wartnose had some food sent to me in the room (it wasn't very nice, and I think the meat was probably rotten, because although the cook had chucked in lots of spices, it still smelled pretty horrible),[6] and then when Wartnose came back up, we had to go to sleep. I had to share with him because there was only one bed.

I kept as close to the edge as I could, but Wartnose was snoring so loudly that I didn't sleep much at all.

---

[5] A midden was a pile of rubbish – kitchen waste, a place where chamberpots were emptied – and where men might go for a wee if they drank too much ale! No public toilets in pubs in those days!

[6] In those days, there weren't any fridges of course, so food went rotten quite quickly, especially in summer. Food wasn't thrown away and wasted, however. The maggots were washed off and loads of spices like pepper and ginger were added to disguise the taste and smell of the meat.

In the morning, however, we were both scratching: the bed must have been alive with fleas and bedbugs, because we were covered in red, itchy blotches.[7] We breakfasted in the smelly taproom on a dirty table that was covered in spilled ale, on stale bread, hard cheese and what was left from the horrible meat we'd had the night before. I don't think it was a very good inn, although Pa had given Wartnose plenty of money for the journey. Perhaps he kept the rest for himself.

And then we set off again. It was a gloriously hot day, but the roads were dry, and the hooves of the plodding old horse sent clouds of dust all over us. We crossed a river at a shallow ford, and the water looked clear and cool and brown, so there were salmon in it, because brown water is a sure sign of a good salmon river. I would have liked a nice swim to wash away the dust – and the fleas – but naturally I wasn't allowed, even though we passed several perfectly good swimming places.

When we arrived at Llancaiach Fawr, the sun was

---

[7] All inn beds were probably full of fleas and bedbugs, but then, so were a lot of private beds, too. Bedding wasn't washed very often, although it was aired sometimes. So the sheets you slept in at an inn might have had several other, not very clean people between them.

almost overhead, which meant the time was somewhere around noon, I expect.[8]

Llancaiach is a large house, set in a good size garden, and it looks well enough to me, despite Aunt Prichard's complaints about its pokiness, its drabness and all the rest of it. It is large and square-looking, and has a great chimney set in the middle of the roof with a smaller one on the left hand side. There is a large entryway with a window over it, and the front door is large and solid, with what Ma might call an 'elegant' pointed arch.

Dai Snaggletooth carried our bags up the path, and Wartnose hammered on the door. Quite quickly we heard footsteps approaching. The door was opened – cautiously and slowly – and an eye peered round the edge. It was quite a low-down eye, belonging to someone who wasn't very tall.

The door was opened wider, revealing a broad flight of wooden stairs on the left and a passageway leading off to the right. It also revealed the eye's owner, who was about my age from the look of him, but who was much smaller than me.

'Who is it, Ifor?' a voice called in Welsh, and a short, dark woman in a white apron and cap bustled up the passage.

<hr>

[8] Watches were few and far between in those days . . .

'Dunno, Mistress Ann,' the boy mumbled. 'Issa man and a boy, Mistress Ann.'

Mistress Ann, frowning, clouted Ifor around the ear in passing, almost as if it were a habit, and jerked her head to send him away. She dropped a little curtsey when she reached the door, and smiled at us. 'Master Prisiart? And Master Thomas!'

My tutor smirked. 'You are quite correct, my good woman. Your Master and Mistress are expecting us.' He was speaking English, just to show off, I expect.[9]

'Indeed they are, sir,' she agreed, still in Welsh.

'Then take us to them immediately, my good woman,' Wartnose said, loftily, still stubbornly speaking English.

Mistress Ann curtseyed again. 'Ifor, take Master Prisiart's man to the kitchens and see that he is fed before he leaves.' She turned to us. 'If you will be so good as to follow me, please, sir? And Master Thomas?'

'The Master and Mistress,' she said over her shoulder as she led the way up the stairs, 'have just

_____

[9] People spoke Welsh, mostly, in those days – but posh people would speak English to prove they could. At Llancaiach, the 'downstairs' people – that is, the servants – spoke Welsh. The 'upstairs' people, that is the Prichards, spoke both.

25

got up from their dinner and are in the withdrawing room.'[10]

Mistress Ann led us through the Great Hall – where maids were scurrying around clearing up dirty dishes and beakers and collecting left-over food, which they would take downstairs for the servants to finish up for their dinner – and into the withdrawing room where my aunt and uncle were sitting. My heart sank deeper and deeper into my boots. This was going to be an utterly miserable visit for me. I'd have Wartnose AND Uncle Prichard breathing down my neck. What if my uncle was as fond of beating boys as Wartnose? I'd have to wear permanently padded breeches, or spend the whole time standing up!

'Sir,' Mistress Ann said, curtseying to my aunt and uncle. '*Dyma* Master Thomas!'[11]

---

[10] Colonel and Mistress Prichard would have 'got up'. Jane and Mary wouldn't have had to, because they didn't have chairs to sit on. Until children were twelve, they weren't allowed to use adult furniture, so they ate all their meals standing at the table! Also, getting up from dinner at around noon was about right, because they sat down for their dinner, the main meal of the day, at about ten o'clock in the morning! They got up in summer when it was light – which would have been very early. It was a long time since breakfast and they were all probably very hungry.

[11] Here's Master Thomas.

'Colonel,' Wartnose oozed, still in English. 'I bring you your nephew – an ill-behaved and undisciplined lad, I fear, but not, I believe, entirely beyond redemption given sufficient chastisement.[12] There are those, I confess, who believe him incurably wicked – he viciously attacked a Minister of the Church, you know, and I swear, the poor man was close to death from an apoplexy.[13] But as I say, Colonel Prichard, given regular and thorough punishment to keep him in a Christian frame of mind – and I assure you that I am here, ready and more than willing to administer such chastisement – he may yet be cured and may even grow into a goodly, God-fearing man despite his sinful boyish ways.' His warty nose twitched in anticipation.

And then something happened that gave me a bit of hope. Colonel Prichard gazed at my tutor with an expression of dislike. He was older than Pa, and his face was much more wrinkled, but it seemed like quite a kindly face to me.

'I am sure that he will, especially with such as you overseeing his punishment,' Colonel Prichard said,

---

12 Whacking!

13 A fainting fit brought on by a blocked blood vessel in the brain.

thoughtfully. 'You have a look about you of a man who would gladly chastise whenever possible.'

Wartnose smirked, but it was an uncertain kind of smirk. I don't think he was quite sure whether he was being praised or not.

'Well, Thomas?' Colonel Prichard turned to look at me. If I wasn't mistaken, there was a definite twinkle in his eye. 'Are you beyond redemption? Are you incurably wicked? Shall I have to beat you twice a day? Or even three times, before breakfast, dinner and supper?'

I glanced at Wartnose, who was scowling at me, daring me to disagree with him. It might be wise of me to admit my sins – but I hadn't attacked the Minister, not really. I'd just mistaken him for something he wasn't.

'I don't think so, sir,' I said, carefully. 'I don't mean to behave badly. It just seems to happen. I'll try to do better, I promise, Uncle Edward, sir.'

'I am quite sure that you will, Thomas.'

Aunt Mary interrupted, smiling. 'Welcome, Thomas. It will be pleasant to have you here, and there will be plenty to keep you busy and out of mischief, which might spare your backside a little. And Jane and Mary will enjoy your company.'

Well, Mary might. I wasn't at all sure about Jane.

Colonel Prichard turned to Wartnose. 'Master Prisiart, if you will please accompany Mistress Ann to the kitchens, she will ensure that you are fed, and then you may feel free to return with your carter to my brother-in-law's establishment.'[14]

I could hardly believe my ears! Colonel Prichard was *sending Wartnose back to Pa!* I tried to keep the grin off my face at the expression of outrage on Wartnose's.

'But . . .' he stammered. 'The Master would have me accompany the boy!' He had completely forgotten his English and had lapsed into Welsh.

'As his escort,' my uncle said smoothly, 'you have done your duty. You will therefore not be needed here any longer, Master Prisiart. I shall arrange for the boy to have the education he needs.'

Wartnose held his hands out, pleadingly. 'But, sir – '

Uncle Edward ignored him. 'Mistress Ann, will you see to it that Master Prisiart is given refreshment? And make certain that my brother-in-law's man does not leave without his passenger?'

'Yes, sir, of course, sir. Will you come this way, please?'

---

14 That is, get back on the cart and GO AWAY!

I noticed she didn't curtsey to him this time.

When my tutor had disappeared, muttering and twitching, through the door, Colonel Prichard turned to my aunt. 'Well, my dear,' he said. 'Here we are on our own with our nephew.'

My aunt looked up, smiling. 'So we are. Thomas, your pa tells us you have behaved quite appallingly, and you are here as a punishment.'

My heart sank again. 'Yes, Aunt Prichard.'

'Are you really so wicked, Thomas?'

I cheered up a little. 'I don't think so, Aunt.'

'We shall see. I hope you will try to behave while you are with us. In the meantime, I am sure you are hungry. Boys, in my experience, usually are.' My aunt picked up a little bell and shook it. Almost instantly the door opened. A girl came in. She was about my own age from the look of her. She shot a quick look at me, then curtseyed, politely, and stood, hands clasped, eyes lowered, in front of my aunt, waiting for instructions.

'Tirion Griffiths, would you please see to it that my nephew is given some food? He has had a long journey.'

'Yes, Mistress Prichard,' Tirion said, meekly.

'Thomas, on this occasion you may eat in the kitchen, if you prefer. Then you will return here to tell us how my dear brother and sister-in-law fare.'

'Yes, Aunt,' I said, meekly. 'Thank you, Aunt.'

Tirion curtseyed again and I followed her from the room. When the door was shut, she turned, hands on hips. 'So? Is it to be the kitchen?'

Wartnose was in the kitchen – he'd still be furious. Couldn't miss that, could I? 'Yes, please,' I said, grinning at her.

She was smaller than me, and a bit skinny, but she had friendly blue-grey eyes under the mousy fringe straggling from her white cap. She grinned. 'Come on then,' she said.

Chapter Three

Halfway down the stairs, Tirion Griffiths turned and looked up at me. 'Is it true you nearly killed a Minister by jumping on him?'

Was there anyone who hadn't heard? 'No, it isn't! I mean, yes, I mean – '

'Well, Master Thomas,' she raised an eyebrow. 'Did you squash him, or didn't you?'

I shrugged, helplessly. 'Yes, I suppose I did. I jumped on him, that much is true. But I had a good reason for it, or I thought so at the time, anyway. I was up a tree – hiding from my tutor – and I saw this man sneaking around the orchard. I thought – well, I thought he was a Parliament spy come to kill Pa. My pa is a brave soldier, you know, fighting for the King. How did I know the man was a Minister? I couldn't tell by looking at the top of his head, could I?'

She primmed her lips and thought about it. 'No. I expect you probably couldn't. Tops of heads don't tell you very much, do they? But if he *had* been a spy, it would have been very brave of you to jump on him!'

I couldn't argue with that. I was beginning to like this girl. 'Anyway, how did you know? I got properly walloped for that,' I said, rubbing the seat of my breeches, remembering, 'and I was only trying to protect my pa.'

'Oh, everybody knows. The Master and Mistress talk, and they sometimes forget we are there. I think it's because we don't *say* anything when we're working about the house, they imagine we don't *hear* anything either. Of course we do – we all have ears, don't we? Although we probably shouldn't say anything, whatever happens upstairs soon gets talked about downstairs – but please don't mention it to the Master and Mistress – there'd be hell to pay if they found out.'

At the foot of the stairs, Tirion crossed a small room into the large, hot kitchen. Although the fire had been damped after cooking the midday meal, the heat from it was tremendous on this hot August day. Above the fire, I noticed a great burned hole in the mantel-beam, deep, black, scarring the wood, and wondered how that had happened. From the look of it, it was lucky that the house hadn't burned down entirely.

A large, red-faced man in shirtsleeves was mopping sweat from his face with a cloth. He looked up as we entered, and smiled. 'Is this the terrible boy who attacks unsuspecting clergymen, then?'

'It is, Master Bleddyn,' Tirion said, grinning, while I blushed bright red. I was getting tired of this!

'This is Master Bleddyn the Cook, Master Thomas.'

I nodded at the cook. 'Master Bleddyn.'

'Well, young man, enjoy your stay at Llancaiach.' He bent forward, put his hand beside his mouth and whispered, 'Better here than at home with that niggly old knave[1] of a tutor of yours!'

Tirion giggled, and Bleddyn Cook gave a mock-frown. 'Tirion Griffiths, best be about your duties before Mistress Ann catches you idling.'

Tirion scurried through the door in the corner, and I followed her into the servants' quarters, where several people sat at long tables eating their dinners – after the family, of course. The family always ate first. Master Prisiart, his face like a slapped backside, sat as far away as he could get from the common servants. I doubt he'd ever eaten in a servants' hall before! He was nibbling at some bread and cheese and looking sour as week-old milk. Dai Snaggletooth

---

[1] A dishonest man: a rogue.

was munching his way through a large slice of meat slapped between two hunks of bread,[2] and slurping cider at the same time.[3]

Master Prisiart gave me a dirty look. 'So,' he said, chewing with his mouth open. 'I am to be sent back to Breton Ferry while you remain. Your father will not be pleased. I am sure it was not at all what he intended.'

I tried not to grin. I even tried to look sad, but I don't think I succeeded. 'Can't be helped though, Master Prisiart, not if my uncle says you must go. I should say I'm really sorry about it, though,' I added. (*I should,* I thought, *but I won't, because it wouldn't be true!*) 'But if my uncle says so, I'm afraid you must, mustn't you?'

His eyes narrowed suspiciously. Dai Snaggletooth winked at me. Then he swallowed the last of his

---

[2] You might think that this is a sandwich – but it couldn't be, because sandwiches weren't invented until somewhere between 1718 and 1792, by the 4th Earl of Sandwich, so that he could eat without leaving the table where he was playing cards!

[3] Cider at Llancaiach Fawr was made by Mistress Ann Thomas, the housekeeper. She had a secret recipe – and always added a skinned dead rat to the mixture to give it extra flavour. It gives a new meaning to 'a full-bodied drink of cider', doesn't it! There were always rats in the Manor – in the attics and in the kitchens, especially in winter, so Mistress Ann had a good selection to choose from.

cider, wiped his mouth with the back of his hand and stood up. 'Best be on our way then, is it, Master Prisiart? Time's a-getting on!'

I waved goodbye to my tutor with a grin that was so wide it almost met at the back of my head! Funny, though. Master Prisiart wasn't smiling at all!

Watching the cart rumble and jolt down the rough road, I felt as free as a bird. I went back into the kitchen and a plump, smiling girl brought me a large dish piled high with cold roast rabbit, succulent, sweet and fresh, and some cider to wash it down. The bread was freshly baked, and the butter thick and yellow, with a tang of salt that stung my tongue and went wonderfully with the rabbit. When I'd finished eating, I wiped my mouth and hands on my kerchief, and stood up.

'You'll be going back to the withdrawing room now, then,' Mistress Ann said. 'Shall someone take you, or will you find your own way?'

'Thank you, Mistress Ann, but I think I can find my way.'

I left the servants' hall and headed up the stairs, trying to walk softly on the stone steps, which is very hard in leather-soled shoes. The door to the withdrawing room was open, and I could hear my uncle's voice. I probably shouldn't have, but I remembered what Tirion had said, and stopped to listen.

'I'm sure he isn't a bad lad at heart,' my uncle was saying. 'But I can't abide that tutor of his. A nasty, weasely character, that man, and no mistake. I shall take care of young Tom's education, and Bussy need have no fear that he will lack in any direction.'

'I am sure you will, my dear,' Aunt Mary said. 'You are such a clever and educated man. But shall you have time to teach the boy when you have so much else to consider? Are you perhaps a little discountenanced that Bussy has sent him to you?'

'No, my dear. The lad has been sent away as a punishment: he behaved outrageously, but I believe Bussy's true reason for sending him here is to remove him from home for a while – great matters are afoot, and it is best that the boy is out of it. No, I am pleased to have him, and I shall make time for him when I can. It will help take my mind from all that is going wrong in the world.'

'The King, my dear?'

'Aye. The King. And this wretched business of the Peaceable Army. Bussy is involved in it, and is pestering me to do likewise.'

Peaceable Army? What was that? What had it to do with Pa? What was that about the King? I was puzzled. I knew that my uncle and aunt had entertained the King to lunch: Ma had been most put-out about it. I think she was jealous that the King had visited Aunt Mary and not her. But why would the King cause my uncle to worry? He was our King, and God had made him King, and that was that.[4] I scratched a flea-bite, thoughtfully. And what was that about Pa wanting me away from home? What could be so important and secret that I had to go away from him? Would I ever understand grown-ups?

'Cousin Thomas, I'm sure you know perfectly well that eavesdroppers never hear good of themselves. It is most wicked of you to secretly listen to my parents' conversation.'

Inside, I groaned. Jane. Dear, dear cousin Jane. I turned, and there she was, neatly dressed in a blue gown and white apron and cap, not a hair out of place. She always made me feel untidy and uncouth by just *breathing!* 'Hello, Cousin Jane. I hope I find you well.'

---

[4] The Mansells, the Prichards, and all the other Royalist families believed in the Divine Right of Kings: that is, the King was made King by God, and God spoke through the King, and therefore anything the King said had to be treated as if it came directly from God! It's as if Queen Elizabeth II suddenly decided that the moon was made from Caerphilly cheese, and everybody had to believe it, just because she said it!

'Very well.' She sniffed. 'But I am surprised to find you lurking here, spying on my father and mother. Spying is not the sort of behaviour one expects from a guest.'

'I'm not a spy!' I said angrily. 'How dare you say such a thing!'

'Oh, I dare,' she said, picking up her skirts, putting her nose in the air and sweeping past me. 'Because it's true. You *were* listening to them, weren't you!'

There was nothing for it but for me to follow her.

She could hardly wait to land me in trouble. 'Papa, Cousin Thomas was at the door. He was *listening*,' she reported.

'I'm sure he wasn't, my dear,' Uncle Edward said. 'Were you, Thomas?'

I didn't want to lie. I try not to tell lies if I can help it – but sometimes, probably just like you – it just seems to happen. 'Well,' I said, slowly, but thinking fast, 'I was tired after my journey and stopped to rest. I *did* hear what you were saying – but I wasn't listening, honestly I wasn't!'

'There, Jane my dear. He wasn't listening at all. He just *heard*, which is quite different!'

I liked my uncle better and better!

'But Thomas,' he went on, 'if you are tired, would

39

you like to rest? I will have Sarah Parry, the Nursemaid, show you where you may sleep if you wish, or perhaps you would rather wander about Llancaiach to get your bearings?'

'May I have a look round, Uncle, please?' I certainly didn't want to go to bed in the middle of the day.

'Indeed you may. I shall find you an escort – someone who likely knows everything there is to know about Llancaiach Fawr. My dear, would you oblige?'

Aunt Prichard lifted her little bell and tinkled it again. The plump, fair-haired, smiley girl appeared this time. It seemed that whichever of the servants was closest answered the bell.

'Ah, Hannah Saer. Will you be so good as to take Master Thomas to the stables, please? Ifor may show him around the house. Tell him to be sure to ask Jenkin Jones for permission, first.'

Hannah bobbed a curtsey and I followed her out of the room and down the stairs again.

'What does Ifor do?'

She smiled back at me. 'Ifor? Well, Ifor used to be a nobody. He was spit-boy and general dogsbody until Tirion spoke up for him. Tidy little thing, our Tirion. She told the Master that Ifor wanted to work in the stables, and the Master listened. So now our dogsbody is rising in the world. He is learning to be a groom.'

I gaped at her. 'Tirion *told* the Master – ?' Servants didn't *ever* tell their Master *anything*, not if they wanted to keep their employment!

'Oh, not in the way you are thinking. The Master offered her a reward for something good that she did – and instead of asking for herself, she asked for Ifor instead. Mind, the Master is a fair man, and made sure Tirion was rewarded, too. But she thought first of Ifor, not of herself, and we think a lot of her for that – although there are those in the Household who are of the opinion that she has too much to say for herself for one so young and lowly. All the same, mind, but for her, Ifor would still be a spit-boy – if he hadn't been turned off altogether, or taken by the constable!'

'Why would the constable take him? Did he do something dreadful?'

'Oh, you'll find out, I dare say. Ifor and Tirion's story[5] it is, not mine to tell.'

To be a groom didn't seem like a great ambition to me, but then I am not a spit-boy. I should think anything would be better than to be a spit-boy. My

5 See 'Tirion's Secret Journal'.

ambition is to stand beside Prince Rupert, who is undoubtedly the bravest and handsomest man in all the world except my pa, of course. To fight beside him for the King – well now, there's an ambition worth having.

Hannah leaned through the kitchen door. 'Anyone seen Ifor? Oh, there you are. You're to take Master Thomas about the place, Ifor, but you're to make sure Jenkin Groom can spare you first.'

Ifor scowled at me, and reluctantly got up from his bench. 'Oh, all right. Just finishing my food, that's all. No peace for the wicked, that's for sure.'

'And *you're* wicked, *that's* for sure!' Hannah said, grinning. 'Now get on with you, and stop whining.'

Ifor slouched across to me. 'Come on then, *Master* Thomas.'

I followed him through the front door and down the path to the gates. He glanced over his shoulder. 'What d'you want to see first, then? The flower gardens? The kitchen gardens? The ladies' bower?'

'Is it all right? Don't you have to ask Jenkin Groom?'

'Don't you have to ask Jenkin Groom?' he mimicked.

He was being as rude and unfriendly as he could be to someone who was his Better – even if I was about the same age. I stopped walking and poked him in the shoulder. 'Look, you,' I said fiercely, 'what's the matter? I didn't ask to come here, and now I'm here, I'm going to make the best of it. Colonel Prichard asked for you to take me round the house, but said you must ask, first, to see if it's all right. So you go and ask, and I'll come with you. Then,' I gave him another poke. 'Then we'll go and look at the stables, not the stupid flower garden and the rotten herb garden and the ladies' bower, see if you've got any decent horses here worth looking at. And if you want a fight, first, well then, we'll have a fight, all right?'

Ifor's jaw dropped, but only for a second. Then his face split in a grin. 'You're all right, you,' he said at last. 'We'll go and ask Jenkin Groom, and then I'll show you the stables. We've got some cracking horses here, no doubt about that, you'll see.' Then his face hardened again. 'But you stay away from Tirion, you hear? Tirion is *my* friend.'

Chapter Four

I was still curious about the big burn on the kitchen mantel, so I asked Ifor as we wandered towards the stables. 'I've never seen anything like it – I'm surprised the kitchen didn't catch fire!' I said. 'It might even have burned the house down!'[1]

'You aren't the only one thinks that,' Ifor said. 'That was Arthur ap Gwilym, that was, who was spit-boy before me. Mind, the ap Gwilyms, they are a lot of lazy do-nothings. Knaves and wastrels, Bleddyn Cook do call them!'

'Did he set fire to it then?'

'Well, not of a purpose. Master Bleddyn had a fine fat hog on the spit, and Arthur knew it would take twelve hours to cook through – and what did he do but drop off to sleep! I ask you! And after only ten hours! A spark flew into the pan of dripping,[2] and set fire to the beam over the fire. He didn't even

---

[1] Big towns and cities sometimes had fire brigades – sort of – which would have been some men with ladders and buckets of water. But out in the country, it was up to the householder to cope with a fire – you couldn't ring '999', could you?

[2] Fat that drips off meat while it's cooking.

wake up! The cook came back and went running to the stream for water to put it out and still Arthur didn't wake up! He did when the cook bashed him on the head with his ladle, mind!'

I grinned. 'Lucky the cook came back when he did, then.'

'Aye. Fuming, he was – especially because he dented his best ladle hitting Arthur!'

'What happened to him?'

'Oh, he was turned off without a recommendation. He won't get work now. Doesn't deserve it, mind. When I was spit-boy, I never fell asleep, not once, never ever. Bleddyn would have skinned me alive and put me on the spit instead, if I had!'

We were both laughing by the time we reached the stables. Now, my pa always says a well-kept stableyard is a sign that all's well with a household. My uncle's was certainly well-kept, and Ifor had a right to feel proud of 'his' stableyard. The cobbles were swept clear of dung and straw, the boxes were new and sturdy, and over everything hung the wonderful smell of healthy horses. One or two large and interested heads hung over stable doors, although most of the Colonel's beasts had been turned out to graze in the fields. Ifor rubbed a soft nose here, patted a sleek neck there. 'The Master has a good eye for horseflesh,' he said. 'He wouldn't buy anything but fine beasts.'

'Ifooooor!' someone bellowed. Ifor could shift if he had to! From a leisurely amble he went into a full-out gallop. He hurtled across the yard like cannon-shot, skidded through a doorway by holding onto the doorpost, so that his speed swung him round. I followed him, more slowly.

'Master Jenkin, this person by here is Master Thomas Mansell of Breton Ferry, the Master's nephew,' he gabbled. 'I'm to show him the stables and such, if it's all right with you, Master Jenkin, sir! If I can be spared, Master Jenkin.'

A tall, thin man sat on a barrel in the middle of the stable, his head bent, showing sparse sandy hair. Harness hung neatly from hooks, leather water buckets stood ready in rows, and feed-sacks and barrels full of oats and bundles of hay were stacked tidily about the walls. A sleek black cat washed her paws on top of one of the barrels: stable cats are always fit and strong – they have to be, to kill the rats! Stable rats are big, vicious creatures. A terrier is best to kill them – they snatch them by the neck and toss them in the air and break their backs – but a good, fierce cat will finish one off almost as well.

The tall man glanced up. He was rubbing milk

into a leather harness, softening the leather and buffing it to a soft gleam. 'Ah. Master Thomas. Pleased to meet you, I am – you'll be the young 'un that's certain death to Baptist Ministers, is it?'

I went crimson again. 'Yes, sir. I mean, no, sir. I didn't actually kill anyone, sir.'

'Well, that's a relief. Verity said you'd arrived.'

'Verity's his wife,' Ifor whispered behind his hand. 'Works in the Big House.'

'Well, Master Thomas, I bid you welcome to Llancaiach Fawr. It's a good house, and the Master is a good man – as long as you don't cross him, mind! And don't you go teaching this young *rabsgaliwn*[3] any of your tricks. He's got enough of his own, without learning yours.'

'Who, sir, me, sir?'

'Yes, sir, young Ifor, you, sir.'

'I won't,' I promised.

'So, Ifor *bach*. There's a good excuse for idling the Master's given you. All the same, when you've done showing Master Thomas about the place, come back by here straight off – Math Mawr needs grooming, and Sioned needs exercising. You ride, Master Thomas?'

---

3 Rapscallion – or tearaway, as we might say!

'Yes, sir.'

'Well?'

'Not too badly, I think, sir. I haven't fallen off for ages. Pa says I'm getting better.'

'We shall see.' Jenkin Jones bent forward and frowned at me. He had a small moustache, and he twitched it at me. 'Can you be trusted with one of the Colonel's good beasts, do you think?'

I beamed. 'Oh, sir, yes, sir! Please, sir.'

'Then come back with Ifor when he's shown you about. We'll put you up and see what you can do.'

'Come on.' Ifor nudged me, and shot out of the door. 'What do you want to see first? I'll show you the horses when we get back.'

'Show me the places you like best.'

Ifor grinned. 'Best place is the stables. I can sleep out here now, to be near the horses. I don't have to sleep in the smelly men's attic any more! Horrible, it is, in summer, all those sweaty bodies packed into a hot room that the sun's been shining on all day. And us young ones have to sleep next to the chimney in summer, and that's always hot from the fires.'

'I'd like to sleep in the stables,' I said, following Ifor away from the horses. 'Anywhere that doesn't have a nursemaid fussing round me.'

'You'll have to get away from the house, then,' he

said, grinning. 'And that will take some doing, I can tell you! Closed up tight as an oyster, night time, it is!'

'Well, it would be. Can't risk enemy spies sneaking in and looking through Colonel Prichard's secret papers!'

'Pity any Parliament spy that got near you! Squashed flat, he'd be, and no mistake!'

'I'm never going to hear the last of that, am I?'

'Probably not. Look, see that tree?'

We were outside the walled garden.

'Tree? Yes. What about it?'

'That's the tree me and Tirion was in when we saw the King. I was as close to him as I am to you, honest.'

'You saw the King? What's he like?'

Ifor considered, tugging at his lower lip thoughtfully. 'Well. Well, if I'm honest, if nobody hadn't said he was the King, and if I hadn't knowed he was, I probably wouldn't have. If you see what I mean.'

'No. I don't. You probably wouldn't have what?'

'Knowed he was the King.'

'What? But he's the *King!*'

'Aye, that's true. But when you think of a king, what pops into your head, like?'

I shut my eyes. I knew *exactly* what Charles I, King-of-England-by-the-Grace-of-God looked like, even though I'd never seen him.[4] 'He's tall and strong and handsome and wonderfully dressed, and, and – oh, just magnificent.'

'There you go, see. He isn't tall and strong, not one bit, and he doesn't go about in a crown and velvet robes, either. His clothes are plain as plain, and he's small, and thin, and a bit wispy looking, and he looks ever so sad.'

'He isn't!' I protested. 'He can't be!'

'You can say that: but I've seen him; you haven't. Ask Tirion if you don't believe me.'

I glared at him. 'I will.' How dare he suggest that the King was anything but perfect!

'Prince Rupert, mind, he's different. I met a man who fought alongside him in the battle at Naseby. He says he's big and tall, and there's not a man alive can kill Prince Rupert.[5] He wears a scarlet coat, all

---

[4] And of course he couldn't have seen him on telly or in the newspapers, either, could he? Cameras hadn't been invented yet, let alone TV!

[5] Mind, Rupert had a bit of a tough childhood. His mum was Charles I's sister, and her husband was Count Palatine, who was chucked off his throne, and the family fled the palace. But no-one remembered baby Rupert! Luckily someone went back in for a last look round, and came across him lying around in a wet nappy, and scooped him up or he'd have been left behind.

trimmed with silver lace and he's so handsome he turns all the ladies' heads.'

'I'd like to fight beside Prince Rupert, one day.'

Ifor looked at me. There was an odd expression on his face. 'You might, I dare say. You being *crachach.*[6] Then again, you might not.'

'What do you mean by that?' I glared at him.

'Oh, nothing. Look. I want to show you something. It's secret, mind – don't tell anyone else. Tirion knows, but she won't tell.'

Ifor bent over, and searched in the long grass on the outside of the garden wall. 'I was pulling up weeds last year – I found it by accident. Here. Look.' He parted the grass, and showed me a large stone. Something was carved into it.

'It's a star!' I said, bemused. 'Why would anyone carve a star into a stone?'

'It's more than a star,' Ifor whispered, as if he were afraid of being overheard. 'It's a *five-pointed* star.'

'So?'

'That means *witchcraft!*'

I shivered. 'It does?'

'Aye. If it's pointing one way, it's bad. But if it's pointing the other, it's good.'

_____

6 Posh – or gentry. Who knows which one Ifor meant?

'Which way is it pointing?'

'How should I know? I'm not a witch, am I? But nobody's died or anything, so I reckon it's prob'ly all right. No witches about, anyhow, not s'far as I d'know!'

I stared at the star. I didn't like to think of witchcraft.[7] I decided to keep well away from this part of Llancaiach Fawr!

Ifor showed me the gardens with their immaculate lawns. 'Not allowed to walk on these, we're not!'

I had to inspect the kitchen garden, and the orchard (we helped ourselves to an apple each, and ate it fast while no-one was watching, although they were a bit sour and small this early in the year), and then the herb garden.

'Mistress Ann makes the kitchenmaids pick some of the herbs in the middle of the night, when there's

---

[7] Which was very wise of Thomas. Many people believed in witchcraft – usually, though, 'witches' were just very old (and probably rather ugly) ladies with warts on their noses who suffered from bad temper. They only had to look crossly at someone's cow, and if it stopped giving milk afterwards, the old lady would be called a witch and blamed. In those days there was a man who gave himself the title 'Witchfinder General': he used to search out 'witches' and interrogate them – torture them, keep them without sleep, until they confessed.

a full moon. She says it makes the medicines work better. I don't know as it does, but it certainly don't make them taste better.' Ifor shuddered. 'I had a bit of a cough last winter, and the stuff she made me take was horrible. It was snail juice. Just the thought of drinking snail juice makes me feel sick. It made me – you know – *go* a lot!'[8]

'My ma says it's better to suffer the medicine than die from the disease. But slugs and snails and stewed rats and mice and stuff . . .'

Ifor shuddered. 'You know what I've often wondered?'

'What?'

'How do they know what cures folk? Doctors and ladies and suchlike?'

I'd never thought of that.

'I mean, how do they know that snail juice is good for coughs? Esther Gruffydd our head chambermaid, she says there's nothing like it. It don't make you

---

8 Snail juice was only the start of it: other 'medicines' were lizards, boiled alive (for the nerves), the skull of a man who had died violently; spit, wee, blood, fat, bones, claws and poo from various animals, birds and insects, all mixed up in a giant pill or 'bolus'. Sometimes they coated the pill with gold to help it go down easier . . . I don't expect it did. Mind you, doctors always very wisely said, 'If God wills it, you will get better.' Therefore if you didn't, it wasn't the doctor's fault, it was God's! Sneaky, right?

stop coughing, like – but because it makes you *go*[9] a lot, it makes you afraid to cough!'

I giggled. 'I don't know either, Ifor. Maybe they discovered it by accident.'

'You mean, someone with a cough accidentally swallowed a squashed snail and got better? Oh, yes indeed, very likely, I'm sure. *Lots* of people go around with their mouths open swallowing snails.'

He had a point.

'Can we go back to the stables now?'

He grinned. 'Come on. You can stroke Math Mawr if you like. He probably won't bite you.'

Math Mawr, a huge roan,[10] had been turned out into the field opposite the house and was over the other side of it, fetlock deep in grass and wildflowers. We climbed the fence, and Ifor put two fingers into his mouth and blew a shrill blast. The great head came up, and Math Mawr ambled across the field towards us. We had saved the cores of our apples, and held them out on our flattened palms for the rubbery lips to nibble. Ifor, his face alight with pleasure, rubbed the long sweep of Math's nose, and put his head close.

---

[9] Ifor meant 'poo' but was too polite to say so.

[10] For those of you who aren't horsy, 'roan' means a red, black or chestnut horse with white hairs mixed into the coat.

'The Master always rides Math,' he said. 'No-one else is allowed to ride him – except me, sometimes, if he needs exercise and the Master is not going out that day. He bit the last stable boy and broke his arm, but he is gentle as a lamb with me, look. I think he knew the other boy was afraid of him. Horses can always tell if you are afraid.'

I stretched out a hand and patted the sleek neck. 'He's beautiful,' I breathed.

'That he is,' a voice said, behind me. 'Ifor. Back to your duties now, boy.'

My uncle stretched out a hand to his horse, and Math Mawr whickered softly.

'Thank you, Ifor,' I called, as the boy set off at a run towards the stables.

'So, young Thomas. What do you think of Llancaiach Fawr?'

'It is a very fine house, sir.'

'I am glad you think so. Now. Your pa has sent you here for punishment, and you may not escape the consequences of your wicked assault on the poor, defenceless Minister.'

I began to feel miserable again.

Colonel Prichard frowned, and my knees quaked. 'Your punishment begins tomorrow. I have decided that, while you are here, you will not be allowed – '

What? I wondered. *No horses? No free time? Extra lessons? Oh, no! Not having to sit with the* girls!

' – to study any Latin, Greek, mathematics or French. You may not learn poems in any language, not in Latin, not even in Welsh, and certainly not in English. I absolutely forbid it.'

A huge grin broke out. I couldn't stop it.

'Oh,' I sighed. 'I – '

'No, Thomas. It is no use protesting. You are to be punished, and that is that. You must take it like the man you will soon be. Now. Come and meet Sioned.'

If this was to be my punishment, I might go and find another Baptist Minister and squash him immediately!

Chapter Five

I ate my supper with Jane and Mary. Mary rattled on about her poppet[1] and her kitten, and she is just about bearable because she is so little – but Jane is a different matter. She didn't stop complaining. Why are girls so prissy and such tattletales? Because the grown-up people weren't with us, we were allowed to sit at table on the benches.

'Sarah, just look how *The Boy* puts his elbows on the table! He mustn't do that, must he, Sarah? It's not polite, is it?'

I took my elbows off, and glowered at her.

'Sarah, look how *The Boy* gobbles his food! Isn't it disgusting, Sarah, to see him eat so greedily?'

Well – I was hungry, wasn't I? All the same, I tried to eat more slowly.

'Sarah – *The Boy's* clothes stink of horse. It's horrid, isn't it, Sarah? The smell is quite putting me off my food, Sarah.'

Sarah Parry, the nursemaid, sighed. 'He's a boy, Miss Jane. Boys are different from girls. They do

---

[1] Dolly – 'poppet' probably came from the French word – *poupée*.

different things. They are often around horses, and if a person is often around horses, well, he will smell of them, won't he, Miss Jane?'

'I think it's horrid when we are eating. It makes me feel quite sick to my stomach, Sarah. I think perhaps his mamma has not taught him how to behave in polite company, Sarah. He should wash, shouldn't he, Sarah, before coming to table with gentle people?'

I'd had enough of being discussed as if I wasn't there at all, and Ma *had* taught me manners – it's just that I don't always want to use them. 'I can go and eat with the servants if I smell that bad,' I said, crossly. 'Better company, anyway.'

'You aren't allowed,' Jane said, smugly. 'You are family. Family does not eat with servants.'

'Pity,' I mumbled, shoving a piece of bread and cheese into my mouth.

'Oh, Sarah, now he's crammed his mouth so full he can't even speak! Oh, how long must we put up with having *The Boy* here? I don't like him. He is very rude and coarse and he smells. It makes me quite unwell to see him behave so. When is he going away?'

That did it. I picked up my plate and went down to the kitchen and into the servants' hall. Ifor was sitting at the long table.

'What you doin' in by here?' he asked.

I plonked myself on the bench beside him. 'Nicer in here. My cousin nags.'

'She's a girl. Girls always nag and pester and whine.'

'Yes, they do, don't they? What use are girls anyway?'

'*Duw*, damned if I know.'

Suddenly a hand grabbed his ear and twisted it, hard. 'Better not say that, Ifor ap Iestyn. I'm a girl, and I don't nag and pester and whine.'

'Ow!' he yelled. 'You're not a girl; you're Tirion!'

Even I could have told him *that* wasn't the right thing to say.

Tirion clouted him on the ear, hard. 'How dare you say that? I *am* a girl! Just because I'm a servant doesn't mean I'm not a girl!'

'Well, I know that! You didn't have to hit me. I meant you aren't like Miss Jane.'

'That's certainly true. I can read better than she can,' Tirion sniffed.

'You can read?' I gaped at her. A servant girl who could read? That was as rare as a talking hen!

She looked at me sharply. 'Yes, I can probably read every bit as well as you, Master Thomas. My dada taught me, and my mam, and I'm very good at it. Sometimes the Mistress lets me read to her.'

'Not often, though,' Ifor said.

'No, but sometimes,' she insisted. 'And I don't tell tales on people like Miss Jane does.'

'No.' I was anxious to get back in Tirion's good books, so I agreed with her. 'That one's tongue runs on wheels – and all of them squeaky!'

Mistress Ann, the housekeeper, bustled through from the kitchen. 'Tirion, the Mistress is ringing her bell. Go now and see what she wants, *os gweli di'n dda.*'[2]

'Yes, Mistress Ann.' Tirion shot through the door, her hard shoes clattering on the flagstones.

Mistress Ann frowned. 'I wish that girl would remember to walk softly – it gives the Mistress a bad head when there is such noise going on. Where is Rachel Edmunds? The Mistress will want her about to minister to her, if she has a megrim[3] again. Rachel is quiet and does not draw attention to herself, unlike Tirion, I fear. And the Mistress is already complaining of a Melancholy Humour.'[4]

---

[2] If you please.

[3] A bad headache.

[4] 'Humours' weren't at all funny. In 1645, doctors and surgeons (Physicians and Chirurgeons) believed that everything that ailed anyone was caused by the Humours of the Body being out of balance. Humours were very complicated, and involved the four Elements (Earth, Air, Fire and Water) and stuff like Blood,

Mistress Ann turned to me. 'Might I enquire what you are doing in the servants' hall, Master Thomas? Shouldn't you be eating with Miss Jane and Miss Mary?'

'Well, yes, Mistress Ann, I was. But Jane keeps telling me how to behave, and nagging at me because she says I smell of horse. So I came in here for a bit of peace.'

'And have you finished your food now, Master Thomas?'

'Yes.' I was puzzled. It was almost as if I'd done something wrong.

'Then please come with me, if you will be so kind.'

Mystified, I left the servants' hall, still chewing my last bit of bread and cheese. I snaffled an apple from the bowl in the kitchen as I passed. Bleddyn Cook sprawled on the window seat, his legs stretched out, his hands folded on his large stomach, snoring. All right for him to fall asleep, but not the spit-boy, obviously!

Yellow Bile, Black Bile and Phlegm. Melancholy (what we'd call Being Very Depressed) was caused by dregs of Black Bile being carried to the head in the blood. The cure was to eat eggs and chicken and other easily digestible foods, and to 'allow only ideas of a hopeful nature'. Yeah, right. In the middle of a Civil War, with the possibility of the Colonel getting killed any day in battle, poor Mistress P is supposed to be hopeful?

'Now, Master Thomas,' Mistress Ann said. 'Back to your cousins, please. You will find them in the nursery.'

The nursery. I'd left the damn nursery years ago, when I was breeched![5] I slouched up the stairs in disgust. Some servants I would have ignored, but Mistress Ann had an air about her that said she took no nonsense from anyone. This was a worse punishment than anything, having to stay in the nursery with little girls. I just hoped I wasn't expected to sleep there, too.

I wandered through the door. Mary was already in her nightgown, but Jane was seated on a low chair under the window, stitching at a piece of cloth.

'Master Thomas, where have you been?' Sarah Parry asked crossly. 'The Master has sent for you and you're keeping him waiting. Run along now!'

I hared down the stairs two at a time, passing Mistress Ann on the way upstairs, and rapped on the

---

[5] Children's clothes were different then. Tiny babies were swaddled – wrapped up so tight they couldn't move, because it was believed this helped their arms and legs to grow straight and strong. Then, until they were about six, children wore long dresses and frilly bonnets – boys as well as girls. When they had learned to use a potty or a jakes, they wore smaller versions of grown-up clothes. Be Very Grateful for Babygros, jeans and T-shirts, kids!

door of the withdrawing room. My uncle's voice called for me to come in, and I shoved open the heavy door.

'Thomas. Come in.' My uncle and aunt were seated near the window, taking advantage of the last of the daylight before the candles were brought at dusk.[6]

'You sent for me, Uncle?'

'I did indeed. Thomas, my boy, I hear from Mistress Ann that you removed yourself from your cousins' company. I can perhaps understand that you are not well versed in the ways of young ladies, Thomas: but Jane reports that your manners are somewhat wanting. I think perhaps that she is unused to boys, and you, perhaps, are unused to young ladies. You must please mend your manners in future, and try not to offend your cousin.'

'Yes, sir.' I said, wondering where this conversation was going. If I could somehow manage to avoid ever eating with Jane again, neither of us would have to worry about my manners, would we?

---

[6] No electric light in those days: there were oil lamps, but they were very smelly and smoky and probably rather dangerous. The Posh People had real beeswax candles – but poor people had rushes which had been collected from the damp meadows and hills, peeled, and dipped in tallow – which was often animal fat – and which must have ponged something awful when it burned.

'However,' my uncle said, getting out of his chair, 'rather than eat with your cousins, Mistress Ann tells me you took yourself to the servants' hall to finish your meal.'

'Yes, sir. I was fed up with being nagged about putting my elbows on the table, and she said I stink of horses, so I took myself off. I hate to be nagged.'

'That's as may be, Thomas. But did it not occur to you that the servants have a right to their privacy and their peace when they have finished their duties? If you are sitting among them, they will not be able to rest, because they will feel they have to watch every word that they say, in case you might repeat their words elsewhere. They know that gossiping could cause them to be turned off,[7] immediately. Even servants need to rest sometimes, Thomas.'

'What?' I was astounded. 'They think I might tattle on them?'

'Why shouldn't they, Thomas? They don't know you. But you are from a fine and noble family, and you belong upstairs with your own kind. The servants will not chase you away, because you are

---

[7] 'Turned off' doesn't mean like switching off the telly. It means sacking a person – usually without a reference so they couldn't get another job, which was what happened to Arthur ap Gwilym after he set fire to the kitchen!

their superior, and they are polite, but they will not rest content to have you there, listening, always. I am sorry, but if you are invited, and only if you are invited, you may visit the servants' hall. If you are not, you must stay away.'

I seemed to have spent the whole time since I arrived being in the wrong with different people. 'I'm sorry, sir.' And I was. I hadn't thought that I might not be welcomed by the servants. Admittedly, I didn't sit in the servants' hall at home – but then, there was no-one there that I liked as much as I liked Ifor. And no-one I disliked quite as much as Cousin Jane in the parlour with the family!

'You are forgiven, Thomas, but remember in future, please. Now. I have asked Mistress Ann to prepare a guest room for you – it would not be appropriate for you to sleep in the nursery.'

I grinned with relief. 'Thank you, Uncle.'

'To bed, young man. You have had a long and tiring day.'

Somehow, I didn't mind being sent to bed. It was almost dark anyway, and he was right – I was tired. I said goodnight to my aunt and uncle, and when Mistress Ann came in response to the tinkle of Aunt Mary's little bell, she took me to a small room with a low bed in it. On a side table stood a large pewter bowl, with a jug of washing-water beside it. When Mistress Ann had gone, I splashed my face. There was also a little bowl of sage leaves to clean my teeth,[8] and I half-heartedly rubbed one over my gums, rinsed with some water from the jug, and spat. Then I flung off my clothes, hauled on my nightshirt and clambered into bed.

Then I remembered a promise I'd made to Ma, and got out again, dropping to my knees beside the bed. I'd promised to pray for forgiveness for squashing the Minister – even though I hadn't meant to! – and all my other sins, although I couldn't think of any off-hand. But then, I'd spent the whole day upsetting people, so who could tell? So I did a general purpose 'Sorry, God', and then I got back into bed. I was asleep almost instantly.

---

[8] No toothbrushes – they hadn't been invented, although Charles II brought them back with him from Paris when he came back for the Restoration – however there wasn't much evidence that the French had used them very often. Teeth were a horrible problem in those days – there were no dentists to drill and fill, and no painkillers, either. If you got toothache they hauled the bad tooth out with pliers, AND without any anaesthetic! Or sometimes they made blisters behind your ears with hot irons, or put strong acid on the aching tooth so that it fell apart. NOW will you clean your teeth regularly and stop drinking so much cola?

Chapter Six

Next morning, the sun shone, and I was woken early by Sarah Parry to take breakfast with my cousins. I was still half asleep, and ate my cold meat, salted herring, cheese and bread with my eyes almost shut.

Cousin Jane was wide awake (of course) and neatly dressed in clean pinafore and cap, her hair combed and her face washed, which was more than I'd managed. She opened her mouth and started yattering as soon as I appeared. '*The Boy* has not combed his hair, Sarah, and I'm sure he – '

'Be quiet, please, Miss Jane,' Sarah said, unexpectedly. 'Leave your cousin to eat in peace.' Even more surprisingly, she did.

When I'd finished eating, I asked to be excused.

'You're to go to your uncle at once, Master Thomas. He is in the study.'

I didn't need a second bidding, and soon was rapping on my uncle's door.

'*Dere mewn!*'[1] he said, absent-mindedly. A small boy, his hair ruffled and his clothes covered in white

---

[1] Come in.

splodges, stood beside the pigeon loft, holding a large bird upside-down while my uncle fastened a slip of parchment, wrapped in a scrap of oiled cloth, to its skinny leg.

'Ah, Thomas,' he said, looking up.

My eyes were on the pigeon. 'Is that a secret message, Uncle?' I asked.

Uncle Edward laughed. 'Not very, Thomas,' he said. 'To your pa, as it happens.' He opened the window and the boy threw the bird out. It tumbled, flapped, caught itself, circled the house and set off.

'Thank you, Wil,' my uncle said. 'You may go.' He turned to me. 'Good morning, Thomas. Did you sleep well?'

'Very well, thank you, sir.'

There was a sharp rap at the door, and at my uncle's answer, a stocky, dark-haired man entered.

'You sent for me, sir?'

'Indeed I did, Bolitho. Thomas, this is John Bolitho, my valet,[2] if you haven't already met him. Bolitho, Thomas is here to be punished, and I should like you to take him in hand.'

---

[2] John Bolitho was valet and 'close body servant' to Colonel Prichard. This meant that he was a kind of personal bodyguard, a servant who slept in his room at night in case Colonel Prichard needed anything.

John Bolitho stared down at me. 'This would be the boy with a grudge against God-fearing Ministers, sir?'

'It is indeed, Bolitho. I imagine the poor man is scarred for life.'

I looked from one man to the other. They were both looking very serious.

'The punishment must be very, very hard, I think, sir?' said John Bolitho.

'Indeed. Take him away and teach him how to load and fire a musket. He is not to be allowed to indulge in any pleasant pastimes. Do not be soft with him. No Latin, Greek or mathematics – none at all – until he is familiar with a musket.'

Master Bolitho scowled ferociously. 'Do you hear, Master Thomas? No lessons, none at all!'

'I hear, Master Bolitho,' I said solemnly.

'If I catch you sneaking away to study Latin, there will be Trouble. Understand?'

'Yes, Master Bolitho.'

'Go,' Uncle Edward said, sitting at his desk, picking up the quill pen[3] he'd idly made while

---

[3] How to make a quill pen: first catch your goose. Then pull out the second or third feather in the wing, avoiding the beak if you can. Scrape the feather with a pen-knife (which is how the pen-knife got its name!), slit it in the back, shave down the nib, cutting the ends sloping. (It would be a good idea to let the goose go, first.) Then, hold the pen between the forefinger,

talking to me, and licking the tip. 'I don't want to see him until dinner time.' He waved me away. 'Go on. Away with you.'

Master Bolitho picked up a long musket from the corner of the counting house, and I followed him down the stairs. In the garden, Master Bolitho hefted the musket and handed it to me. My knees buckled. It was heavy!

'Just point it over there, away from the house, Master Thomas,' he ordered.

I wasn't daft enough to fall for that one. 'I can't point it anywhere, Master Bolitho! It's much too heavy. I can hardly lift it. I need a musket rest if I'm going to fire it, don't I?'

Master Bolitho smiled. 'Well done. You do indeed.' He handed me a stout wooden stick with a fork at one end. 'Now. See what you can do. First, shoulder your musket to feel the weight of it.'

I propped the stick against the garden wall and heaved the massive weapon onto my shoulder. I felt

---

middle finger and thumb, wet it in your mouth and dip it in the ink. When writing, sit upright in a Majestic Posture. Yeah, right. Biros are MUCH easier, aren't they? You could buy ready-made quill pens, but children were taught to make their own – it was probably cheaper, though rather hard luck for the poor goose, who was probably quite bald if it lived with a big family!

a bit lop-sided – I certainly couldn't march far carrying it, let alone wear one of the heavy buff-coats.[4] I could hardly even lift my pa's!

'What shall I do now?' I asked.

'First you must try to load it. For that you will need to put it down onto the floor, barrel end up. Next pour the powder down the muzzle, and ram it home. Take care the powder doesn't blow away!'

There wasn't any wind, but I pretended.

'Now put in the ball.'

He handed me the heavy lead ball and I dropped it down the barrel and rammed it home. 'Good. Now, place the musket on the rest.'

Holding the rest in one hand and the musket in the other, I tried to swing the muzzle of the musket off the ground and into the fork of the rest. The musket was much too heavy to lift with one hand, and the stick was too awkward to hold – my arms weren't long enough! I staggered around trying to put the muzzle where it was supposed to be.

'I can't, Master Bolitho!'

---

[4] A buff-coat was made of thick, heavy leather – which was meant to act as armour. There is one at Llancaiach Fawr in Colonel Prichard's study, sometimes called the Counting House because it was where all the rents from his estates were taken to be counted.

Master Bolitho frowned and rubbed his chin. 'You're going to have to grow, young Thomas,' he said, but he kindly held the rest upright for me, so I could manage.

Using both hands and bending my knees with the effort, I heaved the musket up against my shoulder with the muzzle resting in the fork.

'What next?' I asked.

'Well, next you would take out your match,[5] but you don't have one, and anyway you may not fire the musket, because it would affright the ladies, so you must pretend.'

I waved an imaginary match.

'Now you blow on it to make it burn brighter.'

I blew on my imaginary match.

'Now, Master Thomas, fix in the match.'

I was beginning to get the feeling that perhaps I wasn't quite ready to go to war yet.

'Now, return the musket to the rest.'

---

[5] Not the sort of match you are thinking: one that comes in a neat little box with sandpaper on the side. This sort of match is a length of cord soaked in wee (then dried) to make it burn slowly. It was carried around, already alight, by the musketeers and cannoneers to set off the explosives in their weapons. They carried it over their shoulders, which made it a bit risky, because they also carried the gunpowder about their persons, and might have blown themselves up!

With his help, I did.

'And – fire!'

I pulled the trigger.

Nothing happened, of course.

Master Bolitho took the musket away from me and leaned it against the wall. 'There, Master Thomas. With a little practice you will soon be firing at a speed to dazzle the eye. About twice an hour, if you're lucky – if I'm there to hold the rest for you!'[6]

I grinned. 'I won't always be this small, Master Bolitho, sir! I shall grow soon enough. My mother says that I'm growing like a weed already; she says I grow out of my clothes twice a week. Shall I try again?'

---

[6] Civil War muskets weren't very accurate: they probably wouldn't have managed to hit a target at 60 metres, even! Reloading was very slow, and musketeers would probably get only one round off before the enemy was on them, waving swords, and bashing them with the butt ends of their own muskets. Civil War armies usually had musketeers six deep, so each front rank could be replaced by others with their guns ready loaded. Later, the New Model Army adopted what was called the Swedish method, with three ranks all firing at once. The ones in front didn't get shot by accident, however, because they were kneeling, the next lot sort of bending forward, and the ones at the back standing, so no-one's head got in the way!

'Yes. But next time, don't close your eyes! Now. Take up your musket.'[7]

By the time we'd finished, my arms were aching, my shins hurt from accidentally whacking them with the musket, I was starving, and I'd had more fun than I'd had for ages.

'I think that's enough for now,' John Bolitho said. 'You did well. Tomorrow we'll try again – but until dinnertime, if Jenkin Jones can spare him, you and Ifor might be allowed to ride. So, Master Thomas. Off you go. I shall see you here, bright and early, tomorrow morning as soon as you have broken your fast.'[8]

I didn't need telling twice. I hared off to the stables, where Ifor sweated in the heat as he mucked them out.[9]

---

[7] By the time you'd fired your musket once, you'd not only be exhausted, you'd probably be in grave danger of being poked with a pike because it took so long. Imagine doing all that in a hurry, with people hurling themselves at you, screaming and shouting and waving sharp weapons in your direction and trying to stab you or lop off your head . . . Bet you'd get it muddled, even if you didn't blow yourself up with your powder and match!

[8] What we call 'breakfast'!

[9] Ifor was clearing out all the straw that the horses have pooed and peed on – not a lot of fun in hot weather!

I stuck my head into the box and ducked just in time to avoid a forkful of stinking straw that was hurled at my head.

'Oops! Sorry. Didn't see you there, Master Thomas!' Ifor said, straightening up and mopping sweat from his eyes with a bit of rag he had tucked in the waist of his breeches. He was bare from the waist up, and although he was my own height, he was much thinner – I could see his bony ribs sticking out.

'Master Bolitho says that if you can be spared, you can show me the horses and maybe we can ride.'

'I ain't going nowhere until I've finished this lot,' he muttered miserably. 'And I've still got next door to do.'

'If I help,' I suggested, 'you'll finish sooner.'

He brightened. 'All right. Look, you use that fork and I'll use this one.'

Side by side we worked, and sweated, and got gloriously smelly, wading around in stinking straw. But when we'd finished, there was a good feeling, looking at the spotless stables knee-deep in clean, fragrant straw, nets stuffed with fresh hay, water troughs filled, ready for the Colonel's Math Mawr.

'There,' Ifor said. 'Now let's go and ask Master Jenkin if I can come with you.'

Jenkin Jones was deep in conversation with a lady, who looked up when we rushed into the tack room.[10]

'Here's trouble!' she said. 'What mischief are you up to, young Ifor?'

'Nothing, Enid!' Ifor protested.

'Hmph. That makes a change.' She noticed me, standing beside Ifor. 'This must be young Master Mansell,' she smiled at me, and I smiled back. 'The one who – '

I thought I'd say it before she did. 'The one who viciously attacks Baptist Ministers?'

'Aye, that's the one.' She laughed, and turned back to Jenkin Jones. 'Only a dairymaid, me, but I'd turn that mare out and let her get on with it. Sweet grass and sunshine will soon bring her up[11] – and that foal of hers.'

'Dairymaid you may be, Enid Samuel,' Jenkin Jones said solemnly, 'but there's no-one I'd trust more where the Master's beasts are concerned.'

'Oh, go on with you now. You just like to have your own opinion confirmed, that's all.' Enid Samuel went pink, obviously flattered by the praise. She turned back to me. 'Well, no Ministers about today,

---

10 Where all the saddles and bridles and stuff were kept.

11 Make her better.

so don't go attacking harmless dairymaids, Master Thomas!'

'Absolutely not,' I assured her. 'I won't have time. Master Bolitho said that if Master Jenkin can spare Ifor, then I may have a horse to ride.'

'He did, did he?' Jenkin Jones sniffed and twitched his moustache. 'Have you finished mucking out the boxes, Ifor?'

'Yes, Master Jenkin.'

Enid Samuel sniffed too. 'Aye, and this young man gave you a hand, from the smell of him! Best make sure you've time for a good wash before your dinner, Master Thomas.'

The Head Groom squinted up at the sun. 'Nigh on nine o'clock by the look of it. Off you go, Ifor, and fetch Sioned – I want to see how Master Thomas shapes up before I let him loose with one of the Colonel's beasts.'

'All right, Master Jenkin!' Ifor said, his face lighting up. 'Come on, Master Thomas.'

As soon as we were out of earshot, I said, 'Look, Ifor, can we forget the *Master Thomas* when no-one's about?' I begged. 'I don't mind, honest.'

'All right. Thomas? Tom?'

He got a rope halter and led the way to the pasture next to the house. A dozen horses, some snoozing nose to tail under the trees in the shade, tails lazily flicking flies from each other's faces, stood motionless in the heat. It was the end of August, the weather still and heavy, the sky not blue but almost yellow, like an old, fading bruise. Ifor looked up at it. 'There'll be a storm when it gets dark, I reckon,' he said. 'I love a good storm, I do.'

'Me too. Specially the lightning!'

Ifor was scanning the field. 'Ah. There's Sioned.' He whistled, and a brown and white mare put up her head and looked in our direction. Ifor whistled again, and climbed over the fence. The elderly mare ambled towards us, sluggish in the heat, and nuzzled her white-speckled nose into Ifor's shoulder. 'There's my girl,' he crooned, rubbing the smooth nose. He slipped the halter over her ears and, when I'd opened the gate, led her through it.

'This muggy old weather do get me down, Tom,' he said, setting off down the lane towards the stables, Sioned following obediently. 'I'll be glad when it breaks and we have some good rain to lay the dust and fill up the brook. Just so long as it's fine again, after – with harvest just around the corner, we don't want too much of it, do we?'

The grass beside the road was pale yellow and dry from the long, hot summer, and dust rose in clouds around Sioned's neat hooves. Sweat trickled down inside my shirt, and I could smell the stink of the stables clinging to my clothes. Enid Samuel was right: I'd better have a wash before dinner.

Jenkin Jones was waiting for us. 'Now, let's see you saddle her up, Master Thomas,' he ordered. I fetched Sioned's saddle and put it on her back. The little mare stood patiently while I slipped the bit into her mouth and adjusted the leathers: I'd been doing this since my fingers could manage buckles and straps.

'Well done. Now, up you get.'

I had no fears that he might find me wanting: Pa had put me on a horse long before I could walk. Jenkin Jones watched me guide the mare around the stableyard.

'You'll do,' he said at last. 'You can take her out tomorrow – if young Ifor shifts himself and gets his chores done. He can exercise one of the others – they're getting too fat, they are. But now, Master Thomas, better run along – time for your dinner, and the Mistress won't be happy to be kept waiting, that's for sure!'

Chapter Seven

My days passed in a wonderful blur of guns and swords and horses. The only fly in the ointment was cousin Jane, but I soon learned to ignore her. It was safer that way. I tried to keep out of mischief as much as I could, and staying away from Jane certainly helped.

I didn't always succeed in staying out of trouble, though. I landed in it good and proper when I'd been there about a week. It was early September, and the days were long and hazy with heat and dust. My uncle was quite often away from home, but if I asked John Bolitho where he was, he would tap the side of his nose with his forefinger and say, 'You will find out, young Master Tom, all in good time, I expect, if the Colonel chooses to tell you.' In other words, mind my own business. It sometimes made me cross, being treated like a child and a nobody – but there wasn't much I could do about it, was there?

Every morning I learned a little more – I wasn't strong enough even to lift a pike, but John Bolitho found me a long stick and showed me how to march like a soldier carrying that, instead. Then he taught me the Postures of the Pike which sound really easy when someone tells you how. When you do it in the comfort of the stableyard with a broom handle, it's a great lark – but I don't expect it's quite so much fun when another person is trying to poke their pike into you and skewer your guts with it! The only really good thing about a pike is that it's very, very long, so if your enemy doesn't have one, you can give him a good stab with the business end before he can get close enough to do the same to you with his sword!

I soon learned the routine. First I had to:

Take up my pike (that is, pick it up). That might sound a bit obvious, but not everyone is as intelligent as you and me, and in the heat of battle the ordinary soldier might forget. Which would be really stupid, I think you'll agree, but then, pikemen – well there's this saying about them, isn't there? 'Strong in th'arm, thick in the 'ead.'

Shoulder it – stand up straight with the pike over my shoulder, ready to march.

Mount it – and no, this doesn't mean getting on it like a witch's broomstick and trying to ride it.

81

It means holding it ready to stick in someone –
that is, poking it out in front.
Charge to the front.
Charge to the right hand.
Charge to the left hand.
Turn right about to the rear – to look around in
case someone is sneaking up from behind!

In a real battle you have to march and charge with
your pike, and when the battle is over, you put it
down. You also have to keep five feet[1] away from the
next pikeman in line, because if you get any closer,
you might get yourself stabbed by your comrade, and
that would never do. You also have to hope really
hard that the person next to you knows his left from
his right, because if he doesn't, that could get really
uncomfortable – not to say dangerous! On the whole,
I think I'd prefer to use a musket if I possibly could –
except, of course, that it's such a long and difficult job
to load it. Swordsmanship is all very well, especially if
you are on horseback – but a good pikeman can poke
you off long before you get within sword's reach of
whopping off his head. To be honest, the more I learn
about fighting, the more dangerous it seems. That

---

[1] That's about a metre and a half. Thomas didn't 'do' metres
because they hadn't been invented yet.

doesn't mean, however, that I don't want to be there in the thick of it – sometimes when I am asleep at night, I dream about riding at Prince Rupert's side, and maybe even saving his life. Or perhaps the King's!

Although I was busy being 'punished' in the mornings, I was allowed to do what I wanted most afternoons – and that meant I could escape from dreadful Jane's clutches. She was still trying to teach me manners, and once she even wanted to teach me to dance! I mean, what use is dancing when I'm going to be a brave soldier like Pa and my uncle?

Usually I was off out with Ifor, who quickly became my best friend. I fought him sometimes, though, but the fights never lasted long, and once one of us had a bloody nose, we usually stopped and were friends again. It *should* have been Ifor with the bloody nose – I am bigger than him – but he was like a ratting terrier when he fought, so quick and light on his feet that he often managed to slip under my guard, thump me on the nose, and slip away again before my eyes stopped watering. On the whole we got on – but if I tried to talk to Tirion, he would get angry. I don't see why; she's only a girl. Sometimes I talked to her just to make him angry – and once I tried to frighten her with a huge spider I'd found – but she wasn't at all afraid, so, if I wanted to hear her screech and run, I was disappointed.

This one afternoon, I was at a loose end. Ifor had gone off to market with Jenkin Jones to look for a decent mare for Math Mawr – there was already one mare in foal to him, and my uncle wanted another. There was no-one around to talk to, and I was bored. I wandered away from Llancaiach, and down the road towards the village. I didn't really have an aim in mind – I was just walking, and chewing bits of straw, and trying to make that ear-splitting screech that Ifor makes by blowing into a blade of grass. He can whistle, and I can only whistle sometimes, so I was practising that, too. And then I saw the Tree.

Now, as I've said before, I like trees, and not only for the purpose of squashing Ministers. I always have liked them, and a good climbing tree is hard to find. This one was on the banks of the river which, at this point, was quite wide, although not particularly deep, because it had been a long, dry summer, and in places the smaller streams and brooks had almost dried up. Long, silvery eels were hiding themselves in the mud until the river came back in autumn with the rain. Eels are good to catch and even better to eat. I wasn't in an eel-hunting mood, however – it wasn't nearly such fun without Ifor. He liked to eat the eels when they were cooked and cold and the liquid they'd been cooked in had turned to savoury jelly, but didn't much like the way they squirmed when you got hold of them behind the gills. I used to find one and throw it at him sometimes, to see him jump and yell!

So, as I was saying, there was this tree. It had 'climb me' written all over it, so I did. The bottom of the trunk was quite difficult, and grazed my shins and knees, but once I got high enough up to grab one of the lower branches, it was easy. I went as high as I safely could, and it was cool up there, surrounded by green branches. There was almost no wind, and the leaves barely rustled.

I'd only been in the tree a little while when I heard voices – Very Strange Voices. Voices speaking a language that certainly wasn't Welsh. I listened hard. It wasn't Latin, it wasn't Greek . . .

And then with a huge lurch to my stomach, I realised that *they were speaking French!*[2]

Now this wouldn't have worried me at all – except that I had heard Pa once remark to Ma that

---

[2] Now, you might think this is no big deal – but Britain (mainly England, to be honest, but the Welsh used to get sort of sucked in, too) was often at war with France, and kept capturing bits

with all this bother going on in England, what better time for the French to invade? As soon as I heard these two people, a man and a woman, speaking in foreign, I was certain they were spies. Maybe the French would invade Wales first[3] – knowing that it was less likely to be defended than the larger towns on the south coast of England.

Gradually the voices came nearer, until they were standing directly under my tree!

'Il fait très chaud!'[4] the man said, wiping his brow, and the woman nodded. The man squinted up at the sky. *'Mais on dit qu'il va pleuvoir.'*[5]

Definitely French! I held my breath and tried not to move, terrified of drawing their attention to me.

---

of it and making English garrisons there. One of the reasons English people didn't like the Queen, Henrietta Maria, was because she was not only French but Catholic, too. The Queen had already high-tailed it back to France in 1644, when the Civil War got going, and only came back to England twice after that, and then not until Charles I was dead and their son Charles II was on the throne.

[3] In fact the very last French invasion of Britain (1797) was aimed at Wales – the French arrived at Fishguard, but were frightened off by a large lady called Jemima Nicholas (or *Jemima Fawr* – Big Jemima or Jemima the Great!) who single-handedly captured twelve French soldiers.

[4] It's very warm!

[5] But it looks like rain.

As I peered down through the leaves, I saw the woman reach into the pocket of her apron and take out a letter – and hand it to the man, who put it in the pouch he carried at his waist. The man patted the woman's shoulder, turned and walked away. She watched him go, and then walked off in the other direction.

When they were both well out of sight, and I was in no danger of being discovered, I began to climb down. I must not have been paying attention or maybe trying to go too fast, because suddenly the branch broke, and I fell, and went sploshing down into the river. I came up covered in weed, spitting out water, and soaking wet. My shoes squelching horribly, my hair dripping in my eyes, I set off back to Llancaiach Fawr, fast as I could. I had to warn my uncle that there were French spies about, and then he could raise the alarm. We couldn't let the French fall upon Wales like wild wolves and slaughter us all!

I lost valuable time emptying out my shoes, wringing out my clothes as best I could, but as soon as I was able, I began to run. I hurtled along the road, and, gasping for breath, squelched up the front path to the house, and in through the door, which stood wide to catch any slight breeze there might be.

I hammered up the stairs to the counting house, but no-one was about, then I galloped soggily back down to the withdrawing room – that was empty, too. Jane was up in the nursery, reading, while little Mary played with her horn-book.[6] Quiet Rachel Edmunds was with them, darning one of Jane's stockings.

'Have you seen my uncle?' I panted.

Rachel shook her head. 'Can't say I have, Master Thomas. What a mess you are in! Did you fall in the river? Shall I find you some clean clothes?'

'Never mind that!' I gasped, and raced soggily back down the stairs. There was only one thing for it. I'd been forbidden the servants' quarters unless I was invited – but this was an emergency. I barrelled in through the door and skidded to a halt, scarcely able to believe my eyes.

---

[6] A horn-book doesn't look like a book – it was usually a wooden sort of paddle thing, with a sheet of paper with writing on glued to it. Paper was very expensive then, so people used to glue a very, very thin sheet of cow's horn over it, to protect it, so the paper could be read through it, like we'd cover something in transparent sticky-backed plastic nowadays. On the paper was usually the alphabet, some letter-pairs, like **big A** and **little a**, **big B** and **little b**, and something religious, like the Lord's Prayer or some scripture verses. The 'books' weren't always made of wood: rich families had them made of silver, or ivory. The one I like the sound of best was made of ginger-bread – when children had learned the letter that was written on it, they could eat it!

Sitting quietly at the long table, a wooden platter of bread and cheese in front of her, a horn-beaker[7] full of cider in her hand, *was the woman spy!*

I didn't think twice. I leapt at her, grabbed her arm with both my wet hands, and held on tight. I didn't want her to escape. The cider flew up in the air and landed in Mistress Proude's lap.

She was stitching away at something very white and lacy, perhaps a collar or a nightgown, which got soaked in brown cider. Mistress Proude shot to her feet, shrieking. This overturned her chair, which fell against a bucket of water, and knocked it flying, sending water flooding all over the floor. Hannah Saer shrieked because the water was rapidly soaking a sack of flour, which would be ruined, and the woman spy whose arm I was hanging on to for dear life was screaming her head off. *'O! Trugaredd!'* she shrieked.[8]

I was yelling, too. 'She's a spy, she's a spy, she's a spy! Help me hold on to her. The French are coming!'

Suddenly, into the chaos, boomed a voice.

'Silence at ONCE!'

---

7 A 'horn-beaker' is a cup made from a cow's horn, hollowed out and flattened on the bottom so that it will stand up.

8 Mercy!

It was a very *loud* voice. Everyone stopped shrieking, screaming and yelling and turned and looked at Master Bleddyn, the Cook.

'Master Thomas!' he thundered. 'What are you doing to poor Esther Gruffydd? And why are you soaking wet and covered in weed? And WHAT is all the noise about?'

'I fell in the river – but that doesn't matter! I've caught her!' I gasped. 'She isn't poor Esther Gruffydd at all; she's a French spy! They are going to invade us because the King is busy with the War!'

Esther Gruffydd – if that was her real name, which I doubted – tried to tug herself away from my clutching hand, but still I held on tight. She struggled and glared at me. 'I am not a spy at all!' she said crossly. 'Chief Chambermaid, me, and a respectable woman married to a nice, tidy man.'

Siencyn ap Gwilym sniggered, and Esther Gruffydd glared at him. 'He may be a bit fond of his cider, Siencyn ap Gwilym, but he's a respectable man, my husband, which is more than can be said for you, and don't you forget it!'

Bleddyn surveyed the mess that had once been a peaceful, tidy room, full of people calmly going about their small tasks, and sighed. 'Hannah Saer, better rescue that flour, see if it can be saved from turning to paste entirely. Siencyn, you start mopping the floor, and do it properly. Master Thomas, what is all this *dadwrdd*[9] about?'

I glared at the spy-woman. 'I was up a tree and I heard her talking in French to a man. She gave him a letter. She's a spy, a French spy, and probably a Papist,[10] as well, and I'd wager[11] anything that the French are going to invade Wales any day now!'

Esther Gruffydd tutted. '*Bachgen twp!*'[12] she muttered. 'Me, a spy! There's ridiculous!'

Suddenly, I had a sort of uncertain feeling . . .

Everybody was staring.

Bleddyn Cook covered his mouth with his hand. I think he might have been smiling, but when he took his hand away, the smile had gone, if it was ever there. He scowled ferociously. 'This is a God-fearing household, Master Thomas, and we do not gamble. You have not met Mistress Gruffydd before: she has been away from Llancaiach Fawr for a short while, visiting a sick relative. Esther, perhaps it would be well if you explained yourself. For Master Thomas's benefit.'

Esther Gruffydd sniffed and pulled herself free of my clutching hands. I didn't think it was a good idea

---

9 Uproar   11 Bet
10 Catholic   12 Stupid boy!

to try to hang on to her any longer. I was beginning to realise that I *might* have jumped to a conclusion that *just might* be mistaken . . .

'I am as Welsh as you are, Master Thomas, from the parish of Llangynidr. I have risen to be Chief Chambermaid in this very fine house, and I am a respectable woman and not at all a Papist spy. My aunt-by-marriage is French, however, from a Huguenot[13] family. We are all good Protestants. The letter that you saw was from her, *Tante* Marie,[14] who is still living in France, and the man that I was talking to is also Huguenot, and he is my husband's cousin who lives in Bedwellty. But Pierre can read and write in French, which I cannot, and so he took my letter and will translate it, and when he has done so, we will meet again and he will tell me what *Tante* Marie has written.'

---

[13] The Huguenots were French Protestants who fled from France in the religious wars between 1562 and 1598 because they were being treated horribly cruelly, and being killed, too. Many Huguenots fled to Britain – around 250,000 of them – mostly to London, where they founded French churches that still stand today, and businesses. They became very well respected in their communities. A lot of people have French Huguenot ancestry – including me! My family was once called 'De Lande', or possibly 'Des Landes'. It's so long ago that no-one in my family remembers exactly what it was!

[14] Aunty Mary.

I don't usually blush, but I could feel the redness creeping up from my toes, I swear it. It came up my neck, heated my face like the spit-boy's, and sweat broke out under my hair.

'What have you to say for yourself, Master Thomas?' Bleddyn Cook asked.

'I am sorry,' I muttered. I was more embarrassed than sorry, if you want the truth. After all, she *could* have been a spy, and then everyone would have thought I was a hero!

'We were warned that you might be Troublesome, Master Thomas,' Bleddyn said, shaking his head sadly, 'but since you are a boy who viciously attacks innocent clergymen, perhaps we should not be surprised. Esther Gruffydd, count yourself lucky that Master Thomas did not jump on you from his tree and squash you flat, which is something he is quite famous for doing!'

'Hmph,' Esther Gruffydd said. 'Master Bussy's boy he may be, Bleddyn Cook, but it's my opinion the Rod was Spared[15] on far too many occasions! There's a thing to put a respectable woman through, in the middle of her dinner, too. Troublesome he is. Troublesome Thomas we should call him.'

---

[15] He wasn't beaten enough!

I was quite glad to go to bed that night: it had been an exciting day. Rather too exciting, if you want my opinion. I doubt I shall ever live down Esther-Gruffydd-the-French-spy!

Chapter Eight

I was wide awake, suddenly. My crop of flea-bites itched and itched, and I scratched and scratched, the hot, itchy lumps made worse by the heat in the closed-up chamber.[1] Then I had to get out of bed to use the chamber-pot,[2] and I tossed and turned and couldn't get back to sleep, even though I was still tired. It's hard to sleep when your legs and feet feel as if they are covered in crawly ants, isn't it? I was thirsty, too, so I decided to go down to the kitchens to beg a drink.

I crept out of bed, grateful for the bright moon shining through the leaded panes of the window, because Mistress Ann hadn't left me a candle. I wondered if there might be some sort of drink in the withdrawing room. I decided to look in there,

---

[1] Only one window opens in all of Llancaiach Fawr Manor, and that is in the Colonel's study – to let pigeons in and out. The manor might need to be defended against attack, so the fewer windows there were that opened, the better.

[2] No flush toilets or en-suite bathrooms then! Chamber pots had to be emptied by the servants every morning, although there were a couple of loos set into the walls that emptied into the Caiach stream, which must have been ABSOLUTELY CHARMING for the poor peasants living downstream . . .

first, to save me going all the way downstairs, in my nightshirt, to the servants' hall. Anyway, I was keeping away after the Esther Gruffydd business. I was fed up with the servants smirking.

Everything was dark, but moonlight shone through the windows and a narrow shaft of light came from the door of the withdrawing room, left ajar to let air in. My bare feet were silent on the cool wooden floorboards. Beside the door I could see a small table with a jug on it. I lifted it and sniffed: good, ale.[3] I poured some into a beaker and drank it down, greedily, even though it was as warm as the night. Its bitterness helped my thirst.

I could hear my aunt and uncle talking, quietly, in the next room. I didn't mean to eavesdrop, honestly, but I couldn't help overhearing.

'I am of a mind to join your brother, my dear,' Uncle Edward said. Since Aunt Mary's brother is my pa, by then I was listening in earnest.

'Gerard[4] has been deposed,' he went on, 'but I fear there is still too much remaining unresolved.'[5]

---

[3] Far safer than drinking water, which would certainly have been polluted. No *Dŵr Cymru* (Welsh Water) in those days!

[4] Charles Gerard, who was Governor of South Wales based at Cardiff Castle, and who was Not Popular.

[5] What the gentry wanted, as well as getting shot of horrible Gerard and the English garrison at Cardiff, and replacing them

'I am all of a pother and stew[6] to hear that dear Bussy has forsaken the King and has turned to Parliament,' my aunt said sadly. 'Bussy is my brother, and so I am sure that he knows what is best, but . . .'

'Needs must when the Devil drives,' Uncle Edward replied.[7]

'And you? Shall you forsake the King, Husband?' Aunt Mary asked. 'You have always been a King's man. Will you follow Bussy?''

My uncle was silent for a while. Then he said, quietly, 'The King is bringing the realm to ruin.' His voice was sad. 'I never thought I should see the day when I considered turning my coat,[8] but, Wife, I believe that day has come. There is no real enemy in a Civil War, and there is never, ever, a victor.

---

with Welshmen, was the King's support for the Protestant Church; no more taxes, no more Papists. When the King lost the City of Bristol and left Wales, never to return, the Royalist cause in Wales quickly collapsed. Later, in 1645, Colonel Prichard himself was made Governor of Cardiff for the Parliamentarians.

[6] More or less translates as 'Being in a Right Tiswas', I suppose!

[7] This means that when you haven't really got any choice, you might as well get on with it and do what you have to do.

[8] 'Turning one's coat' means to change sides. When armies were identified by the colours and insignia they wore on their clothes, men would take off their coats and turn them inside out so they couldn't be recognised – 'turning their coats'.

Brother fights brother, father fights son.[9] Everybody loses. If I remain loyal to the Crown, and another Naseby happens tomorrow, I might find myself facing Bussy, trying to kill him while he tries to kill me. The King listens, but doesn't hear: he will have his own way regardless of the suffering he inflicts upon his realm. Bussy is for Parliament now, and I shall follow him.'

I could hardly believe my ears – Pa, changing sides and supporting the Parliamentarians? It couldn't be true! Not my pa, not Bussy Mansell of Breton Ferry! I didn't wait to hear any more. I crept away and back to my airless, hot little room, slipped inside and sat on the edge of my bed, scratching my itchy spots miserably.

How could Uncle Edward say that Pa had turned his coat? It wasn't possible. Pa wouldn't. He just wouldn't. I knew he had given huge amounts of money to the King.[10] I had heard him say one day

---

[9] In fact, Sir Edmund Verney discovered that his son Ralph was on the other side at the Edgehill battle. Because of that, he refused to wear any armour, not even a buff (thick leather) coat, and ended up getting killed.

[10] Thomas's father, Bussy Mansell, gave £30,000 to the King. If you think that Colonel Prichard's Agent, Steffan Matthias, only earned £10 A YEAR, it will give you some idea of what an enormous amount of money £30,000 was in those days!

how much the King's war had cost him – so how could he change sides now?

I got off the bed and paced the room, chewing my fingernails – I'd get beaten by my tutor for that, back home. The room suddenly seemed to close in on me – the darkness was suffocating. I needed to talk to Pa, to find out if what Uncle Edward had said was true.

My clothes lay where I'd thrown them, on the floor, and I gathered them up and quickly dressed, although I kept my heavy buckled shoes in my hand. I opened the door and listened. There seemed to be no-one about, the house was quiet except for the soft murmur of voices far away. I slipped silently down the stairs, and at the bottom, I put down my shoes and used both hands to draw back the heavy oak bolt. The awful grating sound as it scraped against the stone was loud enough to waken the dead, let alone the servants, but although I held my breath and waited, no-one came. Perhaps they were all in their attics, fast asleep. They mostly went to bed earlier than the Family, because they had to be up hours before them.

Outside, I closed the door gently behind me, put on my shoes and tiptoed down the path to the big gate at the front of the house. I stopped, trying to get my bearings. I thought we had come along *that* path, when Old Wartnose and I had arrived, and I set off in what I hoped was the general direction of home. I tried to walk softly – someone might still be about on this hot night – and I didn't know if Jenkin Jones the Groom slept in the stables with the horses, or if he went home to his wife, Verity, the chief Still-Room Maid,[11] instead. The moon was huge and bright, but there were large dark clouds that seemed determined to hide it. The shadows beneath the trees were very, very dark.

I didn't believe in ghosts, but all the same, if there had been any such things, it would be on just such a night as this that they might walk . . . There was a large tree just ahead, and the dark shadow it made was as black as the inside of a preacher's Sunday hat. Even walking on the other side wouldn't have helped: the entire road was dark and I could hardly see my hand in front of my face. I put my arms out to stop me walking into a tree and knocking myself unconscious. I hoped I shouldn't see a White Lady or a Mysterious Shadowy Figure – especially one without a head. I

[11] A 'still-room maid' helps her Mistress make perfumes and 'rotten-pots' (what we'd call 'pot-pourri'), a collection of dried fragrant petals and things. She is very skilled at making soap, which would have saved Col P lots of money.

kept telling myself that I didn't believe in ghosts, not one bit – but I don't think myself believed me, not right then, when it was so dark and scary.[12]

'Where you a-sneakin' off to at this time of night, then?' a voice said, very close to me. I shot about six inches into the air, and my heart almost leapt out of my body.

'Aaaargh!' I said, hoarsely. My voice didn't seem to work. 'I-i-i-for?'

'Aye, who else?' Ifor said, stepping from behind the tree. 'I saw you creepin' past, and I wondered what you were up to.'

'None of your business,' I muttered, and carried on walking – well, staggering, actually, because my legs had suddenly got very shaky, thanks to the shock Ifor had given me.

'Oh, there's nice, isn't it?' Ifor said, disgustedly. 'I thought we were friends, you and me.'

---

12 Llancaiach has its share of ghosts – there's even a webcam set up to keep an eye on them and there are Ghost Tours on Hallowe'en! There are supposedly phantom children playing on the stairs, a woman in a long white dress, strange footsteps in the Great Hall, and a man in a cloak and tall hat in the gardens and on the road outside . . . Want to spend a night there, alone in the dark? No, nor me! And don't bother asking the Servants about the ghosts, either! You'll only find out about them in the Visitor Centre.

We were – but I was feeling so unsettled by what I'd heard that I suddenly remembered being ticked off by Uncle Edward for eating with the servants, and all of them grinning about the 'French spy'. Suddenly I didn't know who I could trust any more. After what I'd overheard, I didn't know which was up and which was Tuesday.

'I thought we were friends, too,' I said. 'But my uncle told me that you servants don't trust me not to be a tattletale, and I'm not allowed to go into the servants' hall any more unless I'm invited. And you don't ever invite me, do you?'

'D'he say that?' The moon came out again, and I could see Ifor's face. 'Well, I didn't know you wanted to, or that I had to ask. Nobody told me, did they? Anyway, I don't think you'd tattle. Some of the older ones might, mind. They don't want their talk to get back to the gentry, d'they? Sure-and-certain way to get yourself turned off, that is!'

I didn't know what to think.

'No, you won't tattle, Thomas.' Ifor touched my arm. 'You aren't that sort. We still friends?'

I made up my mind. 'Yes, of course we are.'

'So, where you off to, this time of night?'

I grinned. 'I could ask you that, couldn't I?'

'Aye, you could an' all. I've been up with Jenkin

with a mare foaling. I come out for a breath of air, and there's you, sneaking past like a Parliament spy.'

'Ha!' I laughed, bitterly. Given what I'd just overheard in the House, that was really, really funny.

'Where you going?' he repeated.

'Home.'

'What, middle of the night? On your own?'

'Yes.'

'Why? Miss Jane ent all that bad, is she?'

'No. It's my pa – '

'What? Oh, Tom, he ent been captured, has he? He ent – dead?'

'No. But – look, Ifor, if I tell you, you have to swear to keep it secret, all right?'

Ifor licked his finger and drew it across his neck. 'I'm no tattletale, neither. Finger wet, finger dry, slit my throat if I tell a lie.'

That'd do for me. That was good swearing, that was. 'Well – I overheard my uncle talking. He said my pa has changed sides and gone over to Parliament. And now my uncle is doing the same.'

Ifor shrugged. 'So?'

'But my pa's been the King's man all his life. He can't change now!'

'Don't see why not. What's the King ever done for you, you tell me that? It's a gentry war, true enough, but all the same what's he done for you, eh? An' all of us are caught up in it, like, whether we wants to be or not.'

'But he's the *King!*'

'So he may be. God might have put him there, but *he* isn't God, is he? He's only a man, even if he is King. And a little scrawny one, at that. And men don't always do what's right, do they? Even kings!'

'I don't know, do I?' I mumbled.

'And if he's doing something wrong, that's getting people killed and making lots of people really miserable, do you go on fighting for him, just because he's King?'

'Yes!' I retorted. 'I mean, no, not if – '

'See?' said Ifor. 'Not as easy as all that, is it?'

Chapter Nine

'So, now then, Tom,' Ifor said. 'You still want to run off home?'

I stood in the warm, soft night and thought. Suppose Pa *was* going to change sides? He would still be my pa, wouldn't he? Could he and Uncle Edward both be wrong?

'I don't know,' I said again. And I really didn't.

Ifor scratched his head and screwed up his face. 'Anywise, how are you going to find your way to Breton Ferry on your own? I don't 'spect you know the way, do you? Besides, there's deserters all over. You don't want to get ketched by them, do you? That lot'd slit your throat first and ask questions after, and that would be the end of you. An' what will your pa say if you pitch up at home? I don't reckon he'll be too pleased, do you? He thinks you're safe out of the way of it here at Llancaiach. And another thing, Tom. If you go home, there'll be that horrible tutor, won't there? You like getting whacked?'

That was true all right. I really didn't want to go back to Wartnose.

'Look, tell you what. Why don't you come and talk to Master Jenkin. He's up anyway with the mare, so you won't be disturbin' him. Honest, Tom, you'd think he didn't have no home to go to, with two little 'uns in it and Verity too. I like our Verity; she's nice. Mind you, his mam lives with him, too, being a widow, and from what Jenkin do say, she leads him a dog's life.[1] Come on. I'll come with you. Jenkin'll know what to do. Jenkin knows everythin'. And 'Cadw dy geg ar gau,'[2] that's what he do say. You can trust him. You know what?' Ifor's thin, freckly face was wistful.

I shook my head.

'Sometimes, I wish he'd been my dad. My dad's a bit fond of his cider, my dad is, and when I go home sometimes he takes my wages and he drinks a lot, and then he's a bit handy with his fists, my dad is. Jenkin Jones never beats me, and pr'aps I deserves it sometimes, but still he don't. Don't you worry, Tom. Jenkin will keep his mouth shut.'

'But will *he* trust *me*?' Suddenly, I didn't know where I belonged. It felt as if the world was changing, and I didn't know where I was any more.

---

[1] Makes him really miserable.
[2] Keep your mouth shut!

'He's a fair man,' Ifor went on, 'an' he believes in God good and proper, I can tell you. You don't need to worry your head about anything. Jenkin Jones will know what to do.'

'All right,' I said, reluctantly. Obviously, in Ifor's view, Jenkin Jones was a man who knew everything – he was his hero, because he understood horses, and allowed Ifor to work with them, and as far as Ifor was concerned, he could do no wrong.

I might as well go and talk to him. I certainly didn't feel like sleeping, and it would be a long, long walk back to Breton Ferry, especially since I wasn't too sure of the way. I might die of hunger or thirst, or, like Ifor said, get caught by deserters and get my throat slit for my trouble. I might be taken for a spy – and I knew what happened to boys who were thought to be spies.[3]

---

[3] In 1643 the Royalists were besieging Wardour Castle. The Parliamentarians inside were amazed when a boy arrived at the gate *asking* to be a *spit-boy*. The Castle Constable agreed, but as soon as the boy was inside, bad things started to happen: a gun exploded when it was fired, killing the soldiers, and other suspicious things occurred. The guards had seen the boy near the gun, and questioned him. He confessed that he'd been ordered inside as a spy by the Royalist army, and had been told to find out about troop strengths, poison the water AND the beer, and sabotage as much of the weaponry as he could. The Parliamentarians let him go, because (a) he was only 12, and (b) he wasn't being paid very much to risk getting hanged for.

I followed Ifor. The stables were fragrant and dark, except for a soft gleam of light coming from one of the stalls. Inside, someone was whistling softly, and making quiet gentling noises.

Ifor stuck his head inside. 'Master Jenkin?'

Tall Jenkin Jones was stooping to wipe down a gangly, big-eyed newborn foal with a handful of straw, while the mare stood watchfully by, bending her head occasionally to take a long drink from a leather bucket of water.

Jenkin turned his head. 'Master Tom? What are you doing about at this time of night? You should be in bed, boy. This is a time for thieves, vagabonds – and Head Grooms, not for young gentlemen to be wandering.'

'What is it?' Ifor asked, bending over the foal.

'Nice little mare,' Jenkin said, with satisfaction. 'With Math Mawr her sire, and a nice-natured little dam like this, she'll be a good 'un, you mark my words. Look at the length of them legs, Ifor *bach*. She'll go like the wind when she's grown.' He glanced past Ifor. 'So, Master Tom? What's got you out from your bed?'

'I told him he should talk to you, Master Jenkin, if you don't mind,' Ifor said. *'Mae ofn arno fe.'*[4]

---

[4] He's afraid.

'Afraid, is it? Can't be having that, can we? Well, sit you down and welcome, Master Tom, and tell me what's on your mind.' He hooked a small barrel to serve as a seat for me, pulled at a piece of straw and stuck it in the corner of his mouth.

I sat, and twisted my hands between my knees, not knowing how to start, or indeed if I should speak at all. 'It's just – I don't understand what's happening with the war and all that. Everything's gone topsy-turvy. Who's right and who's wrong? And my pa and my uncle – ' That was a sentence I couldn't finish. 'I thought it was the King who was right, because God made him King, and so he must be always right, but – '

Jenkin nodded his head, understandingly. 'But you've heard rumours, have you? About your pa and the Colonel?'

'What?' I gasped. How did he know?

'Won't say anything more, but you know what I'm talking about?'

I nodded.

'Funny old world, *boi bach*, isn't it?'

Nobody spoke for a while, and then, 'This war, Master Thomas. It isn't all black-and-white. Some's *for* the King, some's *against*. Being for the King or for Parliament, well, I dare say there's some who've not got doubts at all which side they're on, but for us ordinary folk, well it isn't quite so easy. See, even here in this house there's differences, like.'

'There are?' I had thought that, whatever side the Master and Mistress were on, then the servants had to be, too. I suddenly began wondering about the servants at Breton Ferry. Were there Parliament-arians among them?

'Take Steffan Matthias, for a start. He was born on Canton Moor, outside Cardiff, nobody special, just a woodsman's boy, and yet he got on – got taught to read and write, and that's an advantage not many of his station get. Got himself employed by the Earl of Pembroke, and was doing quite nicely, thank you. But then his Lordship the Earl came a cropper for supporting Parliament, which left poor old Steffan out of a job. So once upon a time Steffan, he was a Parliament man like his master – but now he's here, working for a Royalist.'

'But my uncle *trusts* him!' I was aghast. Was there a Parliament spy at Llancaiach Fawr?

'Oh, aye. Of course he does. What's not to trust? Doesn't matter to the Colonel what side you're on, not really – as long as you're an honest man, and Steffan's that all right, and the Master, he knows it.' Jenkin Jones spat out the straw and stroked his sandy moustache with his forefinger. 'Then there's John Bolitho. He was a soldier, once, in King James's guard, no less, and the Queen's, too, aye. Went all over with 'em, making sure no-one got close enough to do them harm. Then he took a sword in the back at the battle of Ripon,[5] and that put him off soldiering, so he quit. He was owed three years' pay and a small-holding, too, but he never got either of 'em. By then the King had no money to pay him because he'd spent it all fighting the Scotchmen.[6] Now that didn't please our John. So whose side is he on, do you think?'

I stared at him, trying to work out what he was telling me. 'I don't know.'

'Nobody does, and why should they? His business, no-one else's, and he does his job well – even if he is a bit fond of the ladies, but that's betwixt him and his Maker, that's what I think. Then there's Siencyn ap Gwilym – '

'Arthur's brother – him that nearly burned down the house,' Ifor put in.

'Siencyn fought for both armies, one after the other, King and Parliament, and went and deserted from both, so where d'you think his sympathies lie,

---

5 In the north of England, in Yorkshire.
6 The Scots.

hmm? I doubt he knows himself! Number one, that's where his loyalties lie![7] John Davies, serving man, he fought for the King at Newbury, and what he saw upset him so bad he gave up being a soldier and came home.'

'What did he see?' Ifor asked, eagerly.

'Keen for a bit of blood and gore, is it, Ifor? You wouldn't be, if you'd ever seen a battle, *boi bach*, I can tell you. John saw the Mistress's uncle sliced in two by chain-shot,[8] and he got wounded so badly himself he sort of lost interest in fighting.'

Ifor pulled a face. 'Didn't know that, Jenkin!'

'No reason why you should.'

'So,' I said, feeling my way around this new idea, 'there are men on *both* sides, Jenkin? In one house?'

'Not only men, *boi bach*. Catrin Howell also has her own opinion, and quite right too.'

'What?' The thought of women servants with opinions was a new one. Women servants – except for Tirion of course, who was different (especially if you listened to Ifor) – were just people who kept the

---

[7] That means loyal only to himself – he came first in everything!

[8] Two cannon-balls or half-cannon-balls joined together by a chain. It was used by the navy a lot to destroy the rigging holding up the sails and the masts, so you can imagine (or perhaps you can't!) what it would do to someone who got in the way!

house and our clothes clean and mended. They surely didn't have *opinions* – everyone knows women don't think much because of their little brains. It isn't good for them, is it?[9]

'Her poor husband, killed by deserters from the King's army. Slaughtered her animals, too. She isn't what you might call a Royalist, then, but she keeps her feelings to herself. Oh, we all rub along, Master Tom, Royalist and Parliamentarian both, because we have to. And sometimes,' he looked up at me, and smiled. 'Sometimes, lovely boy, all sorts of people change their minds, if the person they are supporting has let them down, or isn't taking notice of ordinary folks, or won't take advice, or goes and takes it from the wrong sort. Had enough of this war, we have, us ordinary folk, killing our brothers and sons and fathers and friends for no good reason, and I reckon some of the *crachach* might be feeling the same. Do y'see?'

I was beginning to understand a little. 'But,' I said, and stopped.

---

9 This was probably the way most posh people thought of the women who worked in their households, as well as their sisters and wives and daughters. Women weren't believed to be able to be educated, and women who were educated were as rare as talking hens!

'But what?' Jenkin asked, yawning and stretching to ease his back.

'But Jenkin, the King has been made King by *God*. So if we don't support the King, doesn't that mean we aren't supporting God either?'

'Well now. That's a good point, Master Tom.' Jenkin paused and looked solemn while he thought. 'But the way I see it is this: God is always right. So if God *made* the King, does it mean that everything the King does must be right too? God made all of us – but that doesn't stop the bad folk lying and stealing and murdering, does it? This King doesn't seem to care how many people get hurt and killed; all he wants is for everyone to obey him and do what he says, and everyone else can go hang. I don't think that *my* God, the one I worship every Sunday because I want to, not because I'll get fined a shilling[10] if I don't, *my* God, He wouldn't behave like that. So I think, perhaps, the King has stopped doing what *God* wants him to do, and is doing exactly what the *King* wants to do. D'you see?'

---

[10] Yes, that's right. If you didn't go to church every Sunday, you got fined a shilling, which was a lot of money in those days! Just think of all the Sundays you haven't been . . . Your pocket money would be taken away until you were a hundred and twenty!

'I think so,' I said, slowly. Jenkin had helped me see things differently. War wasn't some sort of romantic tale, like my favourite story, *Bevis of Hampton*,[11] with persons being shot at with guns or stabbed with swords and pikes and I wasn't really very sure what people were fighting for at all. What if no-one else was sure, either? No wonder people turned their coats!

'Well then, young Master Tom, if there's nothing else you'd like my opinion on, it's time you were in your bed and I was in mine. Ifor boy, you can bed down here by the mare, in case she wants anything in the night.'

Ifor beamed as if there was nothing he wanted to do more in the whole world – I doubt that there was, knowing Ifor and his horses.

I crept back to the house, opened the door as softly as I could, and slipped up the stairs to my room, undressed and got back into bed. My mind was whirling, and sleep was a long time coming.

---

[11] *Bevis of Hampton* was a swashbuckling adventure story, very popular in the 17th Century.

Chapter Ten

Jenkin Jones had made me think and wonder, and over the next few days I kept myself to myself while I thought about it. I looked at the servants with new eyes, thinking about all the things that Jenkin had told me about them, watching them go about their business as if they had nothing on their minds but doing what they were told. The more I thought about it, the more I began to understand. Besides, if my pa had decided to go over to Parliament, it had to be right and a good decision. My pa is always right, even if that meant that the King was wrong. Perhaps God hadn't made him King after all. Perhaps it was just that his father had been King, and his father[1] before him, and so on back to Adam and Eve. Except Adam wasn't a King, was he? Or was he? If there wasn't anyone else on Earth except Adam, did that mean he was King of everything? I remembered the old rhyme –

---

[1] Actually, it wasn't James's father – it was his mother, Mary, Queen of Scots. She was cousin to Queen Elizabeth I – who chopped off her head. Nice thing for one cousin to do to another, wasn't it?

When Adam delved and Eve span
Who was then a gentleman?[2]

Mind, I stopped thinking after that – my brain was starting to hurt! Jenkin Jones never spoke of our talk that night, but he was kind to me, and let me take Sioned out whenever I wanted in the long, hazy late summer days. Life took on a wonderful, peaceful rhythm – days without Wartnose, Latin, mathematics and Greek had to be peaceful, didn't they?

From kind John Bolitho I soon learned how to load a musket properly – although he still had to help me lift it, and one day, when Master Bolitho felt I was able and ready, I was actually allowed to fire it, too. I didn't hit anything, especially not what I was aiming at (a tree), but the loud bang and flash of fire and the kick to my shoulder and the smell of the powder burning was so exciting, I felt quite sick after! Steffan Matthias was enlisted to teach me swordplay – although Pa had already begun giving me lessons – before he was so busy with the war,

---

[2] That is, Adam dug the earth to plant crops and Eve used a spinning wheel to make yarn for weaving. This is one of the oldest known English rhymes and can be dated to 1381, to the Peasants' Revolt. As usual when the peasants revolted, the leader got his head chopped off.

although of course I had to use a smaller sword because a man's one wouldn't have been any good for me. It's no good having a huge sword if you can't lift it or get it out of its scabbard, is it? But I learned to thrust and parry and slash, and gained confidence so that if it came to it, I could at least protect myself a bit.

But best of all was when we took the horses, Ifor and me, along the Caiach Brook, their hooves splashing cool water up over our bare legs. The weather was so hot, I stripped off hose[3] and shoes as soon as I reached the stables, and ran about barefoot and bare-legged all day until I had to dress myself decently to eat supper with my cousins. It was easier to look tidy – it stopped Jane nagging quite so much, for a start, although if my hair was combed and my face was clean, my elbows were usually on the table and *that* didn't please her. Pity the man she marries, that's what I think![4]

---

[3] No, not hose like the squirty thing in the garden – this means his long socks!

[4] Which might be quite soon, and Tom should have felt sorry for Jane, too. Girls were married off VERY young – and girls from gentry households didn't usually get any choice in who they married, either! They might be married to someone about 30 or 40 years older, whose first wife had died, who wanted the money or the lands that the new girl brought when she married!

Ifor had his duties, but Jenkin Jones must have remembered what it was like to be a boy, even though he was so old, and often allowed Ifor to 'exercise' one of the Colonel's horses so that he could come with me in the afternoons. There were sometimes reports of bands of deserters roaming the countryside and stealing livestock and burning and killing people too, and we always kept our eyes open for them, but never saw any.

So we rode, Ifor and me: tall grasses brushed our feet and ankles, glinting dragonflies darted fussily round us like a royal escort, and kingfishers flashed like turquoise jewels along the riverbank. Sometimes we got off and guddled for fish, which Ifor was better at than me – he was smaller and skinnier, and made less disturbance in the water. He let me catch the eels, though! We swam and dried off in the sun, and swam again, our bodies turning brown as the earth beneath our feet.

Halfway through September, we celebrated *caseg-fedi*,[5] the bringing in of the Harvest. Next to Christmas, this is my favourite time of all the year, I think, although it is a sad time too, because harvest means the end of another summer, and all that is left

---

5 The 'harvest mare'.

is a few warm days and then the wet and the cold and chilblains and dark nights when the wind howls in the chimneys and water freezes.

But harvest itself means the end of the growing year, when all that has been sown is reaped and stored against the bitter cold. Apples, blackberries thick in the hedgerow, pears, corn, wheat, everything taken up and put aside until it is needed. All day we worked, everyone in the household (except the gentry, of course, who could not possibly toil and sweat like servants: it wouldn't be seemly). Me, though, I was allowed to work alongside them (John Bolitho said it was part of my 'punishment', but his eyes didn't mean it). Men and women from neighbouring lands came too, to help bring in the corn, as we in turn helped them.

Ifor and me, and Jenkin Jones's little terrier, Dol, spent the morning tearing about after rabbits and hares that leapt from the corn as it was reaped, running madly, the hares jinking and leaping sideways to escape. Some got away, and good for them, but soon we had a good pile of game[6] to take up to the house to Bleddyn and Evan Llwyd, the

---

[6] This means rabbits, pheasants, partridges, hares and other wild creatures and birds that are killed for food.

under-cook.[7] We walked up, hung with rabbits and hares tied by their feet, blood dripping from their noses onto our bare feet. There was a bit of excitement when Hannah Saer screamed at a grass-snake, thinking it was an adder, but she soon calmed down when Tirion caught it[8] and showed her how smooth it was, and how beautiful and harmless.

After, we all worked side by side, the men cutting and the women and boys carrying corn to the place where the great sheaves were stood on end to dry. We got more and more excited as the time drew near to cut the last field. This was the best part, the bit we'd all been waiting for, because who could tell who would be the lucky one to capture the Spirit of the Harvest?

The sky was that beautiful blue that comes just before dark: when it isn't completely light any more, but isn't at all dark either, but the moon has got impatient and is already sitting up there in the sky

---

[7] Evan Llwyd and Bleddyn don't Get On very well, unfortunately: Evan wants to be Master Cook, instead of Bleddyn, and once deliberately mixed salt with the sugar as Bleddyn was making sweetmeats for the Mistress! Bleddyn was so angry he broke his best wooden ladle on Evan's head.

[8] Tirion was taking a bit of a risk here, since snakes of all sorts were thought to be agents of the Devil. The herb rosemary was supposed to keep them at bay – perhaps that's why there's a lovely big bush growing just by the entrance to the house!

like a great transparent ghost, waiting for the sun to go away altogether, and the air is fragrant with the scent of crushed grass and the air wafting with corn dust. All day we had sweated, and drunk huge gulps of ale and Llancaiach cider, (mind, if I drank too much of it, my eyes crossed and my knees buckled, which was Mistress Ann's dead rat, I expect).

By the end of the day, we had bits of straw in our hair, and dust in our eyes and stuck to our bodies with sweat. Some of the house servants were reddened and sore from the sun, having not spent time out of doors to turn brown like Ifor and me.

I was so tired from chasing rabbits and carrying sheaves of corn to the stooks that I could hardly put one foot in front of the other. But when we reached the last field, I looked around at my companions.

Everyone was smiling, knowing that we were nearly done, and this was the best bit. The reapers spread out around the edges of the field, and they all began to reap inwards, until there was only a small stand of corn left sticking up in the middle. This was where the *caseg-fedi,* the Spirit of the Harvest, was hiding. All the reapers, all together, flung their sickles at the stand, and the one whose sickle cut it down was Bryn Llewelyn, so everybody was glad, because Bryn is kind, and is everybody's friend, even though he has suffered such a lot with his wife dying and leaving him with three little children to look after.

So Bryn's sickle severed the last stalks, and he took them and plaited them into a fan shape, and it was taken inside Llancaiach Fawr Manor, to be kept warm and safe in the servants' quarters to make sure the harvest would be good next year, too. Look after the *caseg fedi*, and she will look after you, that's what the old people say. Winter was bitterly cold[9] this year – we had skated on the river at Breton Ferry – and spring was late and wet, but the harvest was still good, so everyone was happy, not only Colonel Prichard.

After the *caseg-fedi* was safe, we went back to the House in a great, chattering, laughing, filthy crowd, and there was the Harvest Supper – rabbit pies and jugged hare[10] and golden apple tarts and mounds of cream and more cider.

---

[9] The winter of 1644-5 was very cold indeed: people were skating on the Thames, and on 11th March 1645 there was, according to the diary of a lady called Isabella Twysden, 'the terriblest wind, that had been known since ever the like, it did a great deal of hurt'.

[10] Not hares cooked in a jug, but a hare cooked with bacon and cloves and mace and other herbs. It's an old, old Welsh recipe – the hare was usually hung up by its hind legs to let the blood drain away, and the blood was used to thicken the sauce. Yuk!

Uncle Edward and Aunt Mary and Jane and little Mary came down to thank everybody, and to take a cup of cider, but they didn't stay for long. I thought I should have been ordered to my bed, but Uncle Edward allowed me to stay up.

After supper Catrin Howell played her harp and people sang, and later there was dancing. Ifor and I held each other up, laughing, to see Bleddyn Cook tripping about on tip-toe with Enid Samuel, but Bleddyn saw us and made us get up and join in the next dance, and we were pulled and pushed and shoved through the patterns of the dance until we were all helpless with laughter and happiness.

And I stayed up and stayed up until Catrin stopped playing because her fingers were sore, and everything exciting was finished, and all the cider drunk and the food gone, and people were drifting away, yawning, to their own beds. Hannah Saer, the under-laundress, had been making sheep's eyes[11] all night at Master Bolitho who was busy flirting with someone else, so he didn't notice, and Ifor was looking forward to teasing her in the morning.

I was tired, but not so tired that I wanted to go to bed. It had been such a glorious day, I didn't want it

---

[11] Flirting!

ever to end. Anyway, I knew that I wouldn't sleep, I was too wound up by the excitement of the evening and the ceremony of *caseg fedi*, and Bleddyn Cook's belly wobbling while he danced. The sky was filled with stars, and the moon was huge and low and had a sort of a halo around it that made it look more beautiful than ever. It gave me a strange, almost holy sort of feeling inside. Ifor, suddenly asleep on a pile of hay, was gathered up by Jenkin Jones and carried to sleep in the stables for the night, and I just – wandered off. Nobody saw me go, and nobody seemed to worry about me, perhaps each assuming that someone else would send me to bed.

I walked away down the long road, no longer afraid of the darkness and shadows and the sounds of the night, not even afraid of bumping into a ghost. Any ghosts that might be about on such a beautiful night would certainly be pleasant ones.

Part of me wanted to walk all the way home to Breton Ferry, and see my ma and pa – I had the energy to do it, that night. But part of me wanted to stay here at Llancaiach forever. I could never, ever, remember a summer when I had been so happy.

I must have been a mile from the manor when suddenly, a deer broke cover and wandered onto the path, standing stock still in the silver light, gazing at me with wide, fearless eyes. I stood silent and motionless, scarcely able to breathe, watching her. She was like a creature from magic, conjured up by Merlin the Magician.[12] She could have been a unicorn with a single silver horn and delicate silver hooves, haloed by the moonlight . . .

Suddenly, her ears flicked, her body tensed, and she sprang into the trees lining the road, and was gone. What had frightened her? It hadn't been me – I'd kept still as a stone.

I listened, and my ears finally heard what her keener ones had heard long before. Voices.

---

[12] Yes, Thomas would have known all about Merlin and King Arthur and Lancelot and all the rest of them – those stories are very, very old.

Chapter Eleven

I listened hard: I could hear voices, but I couldn't make out what they were saying: they were speaking too quietly. I thought perhaps I'd caught someone from the Manor, a man and a girl, kissing and cuddling. I decided I'd spy on them, then I could tease them tomorrow!

But no: they were harsh men's voices, and clinking metal, the muffled whinny of a horse, the low growl of a dog, swiftly hushed.

Sweat broke out all over me, and yet I was cold with terror. There were no armies around Llancaiach, I was sure of that, but I knew there were deserters roaming the countryside, from both Royalist and Parliamentarian armies. I knew what happened to people who were caught by deserters.[1]

---

[1] A five-year-old boy was on his way to join his father, an officer in the Royalist army, in Oxford. An escort went with him, but he was only young himself, and some deserters caught them and stole all their clothes and money, even the clothes they were wearing, so he and the little boy had to beg for food to get them to Oxford. What sort of a person would do something like that to a child?

And Catrin Howell's husband had been killed by deserters – from the King's army! I didn't want that to happen to me. And if it wasn't deserters, it might even be pirates – I had heard stories of the ferocious things the Barbary pirates did, too.[2] I didn't want to be found by either of them, deserters *or* pirates.

I looked frantically around to find a place to hide. No good hiding in the undergrowth – they had a dog, and it would sniff me out straight away.

As you know, I've always been a good climber, and there was a tree a little way ahead that looked as if it might be easy to climb and good to hide in. Walking as quietly as I could, I made for the tree, my heart thumping. I kicked off my shoes, and began to climb. Up and up I went, until I was high in the branches, and completely concealed by the leaves and the darkness. Then I realised my mistake . . .

I'd left my shoes at the bottom: smelly shoes, because I'd been working in them all day. If a dog

---

[2] Believe it or not, Barbary pirates from the north coast of Africa were a big problem, even in Wales. They landed on the Scilly Isles off Cornwall, and made the local people's lives so miserable that they all ran away and left the islands to the pirates, who used to harry the west coast of Great Britain and rob and plunder and lots of swashbuckly stuff like that. Forget Pirates of the Caribbean – this was Pirates of the English Channel!

got wind of them – and didn't die from the smell – it would certainly find me, hidden in the tree.

I should just have to take my chances and stay put. I shut my eyes and said some prayers, quick.

The horsemen were getting closer, still riding slowly and as silently as a large group of horsemen was able. When they were right under the tree, I cautiously parted the leaves and peered down. Moonlight glinted on musket-muzzles, on pikes, on horse-harness and the hilts of swords. Buff-coats were tied over saddles because of the heat. The men bristled with weapons, but they didn't look like soldiers. They were dirty and ragged and it seemed no-one was commanding them. Deserters – and heading for Llancaiach.

I thought of the peaceful Manor, silent in the moonlight, where unsuspecting people were heavily asleep after the *caseg-fedi* and dancing and Mistress Ann's rat cider. On this special night, what if no-one was on guard? What if they attacked the stables to steal Uncle Edward's horses? They might kill poor Ifor, because it was certain he wouldn't let them take any of his beloved horses without a fight, and Ifor wasn't big enough to fight a grown man – although he'd certainly try. He'd fight with the ferocity of a terrier – except that these human rats were bigger and more dangerous than any stable rat. Ifor would certainly be killed.

Luckily, the dogs must have found more interesting things to smell than my stinky shoes. As soon as the riders were past me and a little way down the road, I shinned down the tree like a Barbary ape and began to run – like the wind, not bothering to scramble into shoes, cutting my bare feet on sticks and stones, torn by brambles, stung by nettles, tripping over unseen tree-roots. I didn't dare run down the middle of the road – when I got level with the band of horsemen, I crept past them, silently flitting from tree to tree like a wild savage from the New World, with feathers in my hair.[3]

By the time I reached the stableyard, my heart was trying to jump out of my chest, I had a stitch in my side and there was no time to bend over to ease it: I could barely breathe from the pain of the running. I hurtled across the cobbles and crashed into the stable. The moon slid in after me and made it bright as day.

Ifor was curled on the straw with his thumb in his mouth – I should remember that, to tease him, later – if we survived!

---

[3] A Native American Indian.

'Ifor, wake up!' I gasped.

He mumbled and turned over. I fell to my knees and shook him, hard. He mumbled something *very* rude.

'Ifor, you have to wake up!'

He opened a bleary eye. '*Beth sy?*'[4]

'Keep your voice down,' I hissed. 'There's men coming, with muskets and swords, heading for Llancaiach. We've got to raise the alarm, quick or they'll all be murdered in their beds!'

He sat up, and rubbed his eyes. 'You're having me on, Thomas. Go away. I'm too tired. You and your stupid jokes.' He lay back down again, and shut his eyes.

'It's not a joke, it's not! Ifor, wake up! You've got to help me!'

'*Wir?*'[5]

'*Wir!*'

At last he was properly awake. He knuckled the sleep from his eyes, scrambled to his feet and hared through the stable door. He galloped down the path to the Big House, skidded round the corner into the garden, raced up the path and hammered on the front door. Fearing that even the sound of the

---

[4] What's the matter?
[5] Honest?

massive knocker wasn't going to be enough, I ripped up a large stone bordering the path and used that to bash with, hammering stone on wood until the crashes and thuds resounded inside the house. Surely someone would hear us now! I prayed that not all the servants would be sleeping in the attics – if only *some* had fallen asleep in the kitchen. I hoped that they hadn't drunk so much of Mistress Ann's cider that they wouldn't hear us knocking.

'Help!' I yelled. 'Wake up, quick!' At long last there were stumbling footsteps in the hall, and the heavy bars inside were lifted and the bolt drawn back. The door opened, and a bleary eye looked out. Siencyn ap Gwilym, much the worse for wear[6] after the Harvest Supper, scowled at us.

'Wass all the noise about, Ifor? You'll get my hand acrost yer ear if you don't stop your banging!'

Ifor pushed past him, knocking him flat. I followed, jumping over Siencyn, struggling helplessly on his back like a black beetle, his arms and legs waving in the air. We pounded up the stairs towards my uncle's chamber, yelling all the way. John Bolitho was already up from his little truckle bed beside Uncle Edward's, and was at the door in his nightshirt, a candle in his hand.

---

[6] That is, he'd probably drunk too much Rat Cider!

'What is this noise?' he hissed angrily. 'Master Thomas, you will wake your uncle! Is this another of your – '

'Oh, Master Bolitho, quick, come quick. We have to wake everyone. There's a whole lot of men coming with swords and muskets and things. I think they must be deserters, and they aren't very far away at all!' I bleated, my voice (which sometimes sounds quite deep) squeaking like little Mary's. 'Oh, quick, Master Bolitho, or they will murder us all! They'll be here any minute!'

John Bolitho moved like lightning, and was pulling on his breeches in a second, rousing the Colonel, shouting all the while for the other servants, who tumbled from odd corners and doorways, dressing and arming themselves with anything they could lay their hands on.

John Bolitho handed out muskets, shot and powder, and Steffan Matthias handed out the long pikes that stood in the corner of the counting house. When every man was armed with something – even if it was a poker, a kitchen ladle, or a hay-fork, they set out from the house. Bleddyn Cook was left to bolt the door behind them and stand guard over the women, who twittered like silly birds in the hall, certain they were about to be murdered. Mary was snuggling sleepily into Rachel Edmunds's shoulder, not understanding what was happening, but Jane was clutching Mistress Ann's sleeve and shrieking. Trust Jane to make a fuss.

'Best stay behind, lads,' one of the servants said to Ifor and me – but he didn't wait around to make sure we obeyed, so we didn't! We followed along behind the men, Ifor clutching a pitchfork, me armed with the stick that John Bolitho used to prop up the musket.

Oh, it was the most exciting thing in my life, ever at all! Our men crept silently through the trees until they had completely surrounded the slow-moving column, and then, at my uncle's shout, they attacked the ragtag deserters. There was a lot of very loud yelling, cursing and swearing and oaths and blasphemies (Ifor and me learned some new ones) and groans and screams and cries from people who were wounded, and a great clangour of steel. Sparks flew from swords clashing in the darkness, and despite the confusion and excitement, someone managed to load and fire a musket. The ball went straight into a tree and terrified a barn owl and a crowd of bats, which shot out in panic. It didn't take long to disarm the deserters and round them up. They were tied up in a long line, their horses taken back to Llancaiach, and they themselves were locked up in the barn overnight, under guard, until they could be marched off to the constable in Bedwellty to be Dealt With. Only Siencyn ap Gwilym had been wounded, and that was in his bum. He got teased a lot by the other servants, who said that it was typical – he had obviously been running away again!

Back at the House I was sent to bed, no arguing, and although my ears rang with excitement, I went, and fell asleep sideways across the bed with all my clothes on, except my shoes, which were still under the tree.

I slept until dinner time next day – gone half-past ten – and no-one came to wake me. When I stumbled, bleary-eyed and barefoot from my chamber, I was sent to the kitchens for food. I was patted on the back by all the men, who swore I'd saved their lives, and hugged by all the women, which I didn't enjoy at all, except when Tirion did it. I like Tirion, and I would have hugged her back, but everybody was watching, especially Ifor who, even if he is my friend, thinks Tirion is his property and no-one else should even speak to her, and especially not me.

That afternoon, Ifor and I were Sent For. Hannah Saer grabbed Ifor and scrubbed his face with a wet cloth, and spat on her hands to try to make his hair lie flat, but it wouldn't: it just stuck up in damp clumps. She looked as if she'd like to do the same to me, but I gave her a Very Stern Look, so she didn't.

Uncle Edward was in his counting house. 'Young Thomas,' he said, 'I am proud of you. Your Brave and Timely Action saved us all from being murdered in our beds!' I went bright red, and hoped he'd tell Pa (he did, later). He gave Ifor a whole twopence, and Ifor was speechless with pride and pleasure! He spent the money ten times over, in his head, before he went to bed that night.

John Bolitho was there, too, and Steffan Matthias, and they both shook my hand and Ifor's too, but they didn't give him anything, although I noticed Master Matthias speaking to him a little more kindly, after, than he sometimes did, as if Ifor had earned his respect.

'Well, Thomas,' Uncle Edward smiled at me. 'Your pa would be proud of you. What do you think? Have you been punished enough? Will you continue to be Troublesome, Thomas? Shall you go home tomorrow, Thomas?'

I started to smile. I could tell he was teasing. Then I stopped smiling. My face drooped miserably. I wanted to go back to Breton Ferry, see my pa and my ma, but . . .

My uncle looked alarmed. 'What is it, Thomas?'

Breton Ferry. Old Wartnose. Latin. Greek. Mathematics. No more rides in the sunshine with Ifor, no more cool splashing in streams, no nights in the fragrant stable talking to Jenkin Jones.

'Do I have to go home just yet?' I begged. 'Mayn't I stay a little longer?'

My uncle frowned. 'Hmm. Well.'

'I think I've still got some Troublesome in me, Uncle Edward.' I pulled a face. 'What if I attack another Minister, Uncle?' I held my breath.

'Oh,' he said at last. 'Hmm.' Then, 'Do you think you might?'

I crossed my fingers behind my back and nodded.

Uncle Edward shook his head, but he was smiling. 'Perhaps you *do* need to stay a while longer, or there won't be a Minister safe in the whole of Wales. But – '

'Yes, Uncle Edward?'

'Try not to be *too* Troublesome, Thomas!'

Author's End Note . . .

or

What happened to old Charlie, then?

Although Charles I was probably the main cause of the Civil War, you have to feel a bit sorry for him. He was James I's second son and third child, and his big brother was, of course, the heir to the throne – although he died later, which is why Charles became king instead. Charles wasn't anyone's favourite, and was a bit neglected. He was passed over to a posh lady to be taken care of, and also had a wet-nurse (someone who breastfed him instead of his own mum) and a cradle-rocker. When Queen Elizabeth I died, James VI of Scotland became James I of England, and he and his wife left Scotland and left Charles behind, although their other children followed later.

Poor Charles was very bright, but his body was weak – he suffered from rickets, which affected his spine and breastbone. Sufferers don't grow very tall, and tend to have bad teeth and bandy legs. So Charles was scrawny and weak, and was bullied by just about everybody. Perhaps if someone had loved him lots when he was little, he wouldn't have got himself into such trouble when he became king. He used to have screaming tantrums (no wonder!) when he was a child, and when he grew up he kept right on having them. He was brought up by all sorts of different people, but I doubt if any of them loved him as much as children ought to be loved.

His enemy Oliver Cromwell, however, was born into an East Anglian gentry family, although not a rich one. He was the only boy in a big family of girls, so he was probably spoiled rotten, and when he grew up, was a very Confident Person because of it.

People in those days believed in omens – which were sort of signals of bad luck. Anything could be an omen – a crow on a chimney pot, a big storm or shooting star. The omens for Charles setting out to war were blooming awful. When he tried to raise his standard,[1] it was pouring with rain, for a start, and it had to be planted in a hole scraped out of the mud, so that it blew down in the night and got soggy and messy. A wiser man than Charles I might have thought, 'Oh, blow this for a game of soldiers!' and gone straight home, but Charles was never very wise, unfortunately.

---

[1] Which in this case doesn't mean getting better at something – it means flying the Royal Flag at the head of his troops.

Unusually for Royals in those times (because their husbands and wives were usually chosen for them by their parents, or even worse, by politicians), Charles and his French wife, Henrietta Maria, dearly loved each other. Because Charles was afraid for her safety, he sent his wife off to France in 1644. She was expecting a baby, which she had at Exeter on the way to the boat, but she left the tiny girl behind when she sailed, because crossing the Channel was dangerous in those days. (Don't worry, the baby was well looked after!)

Lots of Royalist strongholds started to surrender in 1645, when everything at Llancaiach happens, and when he lost the Battle of Naseby, King Charles fled to Raglan Castle in Monmouthshire, where he had a jolly nice sort of a three-week holiday from fighting and war and everything. There was bowling on the green, and other sports, and lots of entertainment, and I expect the weather was quite nice and perhaps he even sunbathed a bit while he ambled round the moat on the walk with the statues set in the wall-niches.[2]

Then things got worse, and it never really got

---

[2] The niches are still there – they were lined with sea-shells, and you can still see traces of them if you look closely – but the statues have been taken away.

much better, afterwards: his younger son James escaped dressed in girls' clothes, and his son and the heir to the throne of England, Charles II, escaped by hiding in oak trees[3] and stuff. They fled to France, and Charles I ended up running back to Scotland for protection. He kept writing to his wife in France, asking if he could please give up and not be king any more, but she kept writing back and saying 'Pull yourself together, man!' and 'Don't you dare – think of the children!' to him, so he didn't. Henrietta Maria never dreamed that one day her husband's head might be chopped off. She thought he just had to be Very Firm with people and everything would be all right again. Charles thought he'd be safe in Scotland, but he'd managed to upset them, too, by trying to force a different prayer book on them, so they handed him over to Parliament in January 1647.

Charles was imprisoned for a time in Carisbrooke Castle on the Isle of Wight, and tried to escape. But – just his luck – he was trying to wriggle through the bars on the windows of his bedroom: his head went through, but the rest of him got stuck, and he had to struggle back into the room. I expect he felt a bit silly about that.

---

[3] Only one actually, the Boscobel Oak!

And then, in 1649 Charles was taken to Whitehall, in London, to be tried for high treason. Charles still didn't believe that anyone would dare to try a person for treason who had been made king by God, and when the prosecutor was reading the indictment[4] he kept whacking him on the shoulder with his silver-topped walking-cane to try to interrupt him so he could argue. Eventually the silver top fell off, and Charles looked around crossly, waiting for someone to pick it up, and bow, and hand it to him. *But nobody did!* Some people think that this might have been the first time that Charles actually realised that he was in Dead Trouble.

Well, he was tried and condemned to death by having his head chopped off with an axe. The night before the execution he was allowed to say goodbye to his two younger children (but not the new baby, Henrietta-Maria-after-her-mam-but-usually-known-as-Minette. He never even saw her). He told the eight-year-old boy that whatever anyone said to him, or promised him, he must *never* allow himself to be made king while his brothers Charles and James were still alive (they were safe in France). The

---

[4] This means, the stuff that they were saying Charles had done, that made him be Treasonous.

poor children – Elizabeth, who understood what was happening because she was a bit older, and the little boy, Henry – were led away in floods of tears, never to see their papa again.

Next day, on 30 January 1649, Charles was taken out through a window of Whitehall Palace onto a scaffold to be executed. It was a very cold morning, and Charles put on two shirts so that he wouldn't shiver with cold – he didn't want anyone to think he was trembling with fear. He tucked his long hair under a white satin nightcap so it wouldn't get in the way of the axe, made a very short speech followed by the single word, 'Remember!' (although no-one was quite sure what he meant by it). Then he prayed a little, lay down by the block and stretched out his arms and – whack. Down came the axe: no more Charles I.

By the time Charles II came along, Oliver Cromwell had already died – so he was dug up and his head displayed on a spike in revenge!

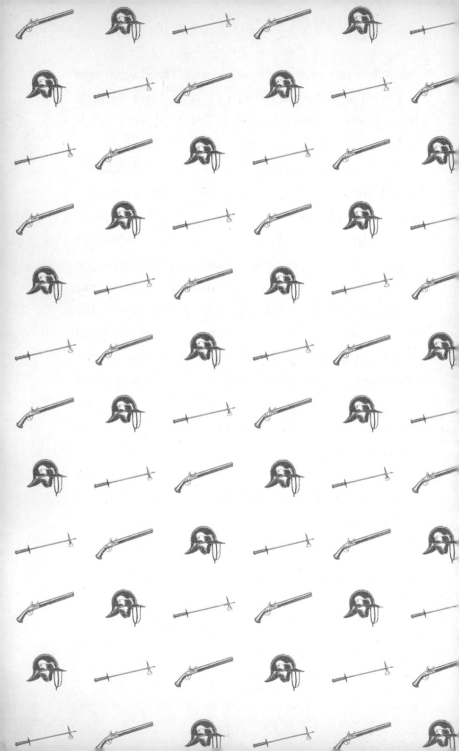